BLIX

BY FRANK NORRIS

Blix
Moran of the Lady Letty
The Octopus
The Pit

BLIX

FRANK NORRIS

WILDSIDE PRESS: MMIII

BLIX

Published by
Wildside Press
P.O. Box 301
Holicong, PA 18928-0301 USA
www.wildsidepress.com

Chapter I

IT had just struck nine from the cuckoo clock that hung over the mantelpiece in the dining-room, when Victorine brought in the halved watermelon and set it in front of Mr. Bessemer's plate. Then she went down to the front door for the damp, twisted roll of the Sunday morning's paper, and came back and rang the breakfast-bell for the second time.

As the family still hesitated to appear, she went to the bay window at the end of the room, and stood there for a moment looking out. The view was wonderful. The Bessemers lived upon the Washington Street hill, almost at its very summit, in a flat in the third story of the building. The contractor had been clever enough to reverse the position of kitchen and dining-room, so that the latter room was at the rear of the house. From its window one could command a sweep of San Francisco Bay and the Contra Costa shore, from Mount Diablo, along past Oakland, Berkeley, Sausalito, and Mount Tamalpais, out to the Golden Gate, the Presidio, the ocean, and even—on very clear days—to the Farrallone islands.

For some time Victorine stood looking down at the great expanse of land and sea, then faced about with an impatient exclamation.

On Sundays all the weekday regime of the family was deranged, and breakfast was a movable feast, to be had any time after seven or before half-past nine. As Victorine was pouring the icewater, Mr. Bessemer himself came in, and addressed himself at once to his meal, without so much as a thought of waiting for the others.

He was a little round man. He wore a skullcap to keep his bald spot warm, and read his paper through a reading-glass. The expression of his face, wrinkled and bearded, the eyes shadowed by enormous gray eyebrows, was that of an amiable gorilla.

Bessemer was one of those men who seem entirely disassociated from their families. Only on rare and intense occasions did his paternal spirit or instincts assert themselves. At table he talked but little. Though devotedly fond of his eldest daughter, she was a puzzle and a stranger to him. His interests and hers were absolutely dissimilar. The children he seldom spoke to but to reprove; while Howard, the son, the ten-year-old and terrible infant of the household, he always referred to as "that boy."

He was an abstracted, self-centered old man, with but two hobbies—homoeopathy and the mechanism of clocks. But he had a strange way of talking to himself in a low voice, keeping up a running, half-whispered comment upon his own doings and actions; as, for instance, upon this occasion: "Nine o'clock—the clock's a little fast. I think I'll wind my watch. No, I've forgotten my watch. Watermelon this morning, eh? Where's a knife? I'll have a little salt. Victorine's forgot the spoons—ha, here's a spoon! No, it's a knife I want."

After he had finished his watermelon, and while Victorine was pouring his coffee, the two children came in, scrambling to their places, and drumming on the table with their knife-handles.

The son and heir, Howard, was very much a boy. He played baseball too well to be a very good boy, and for the sake of his own self-respect maintained an attitude of perpetual revolt against his older sister, who, as much as possible, took the place of the mother, long since dead. Under her supervision, Howard blacked his own shoes every morning before breakfast, changed his underclothes twice a week, and was dissuaded from playing with the dentist's son who lived three doors below and who had St. Vitus' dance.

His little sister was much more tractable. She had been christened Alberta, and was called Snooky. She promised to be pretty when she grew up, but was at this time in that distressing transitional stage between twelve and fifteen; was long-legged, and endowed with all the awkwardness of a colt. Her shoes were still innocent of heels; but on those occasions when she was allowed to wear her tiny first pair of corsets she was exalted to an almost celestial pitch of silent ecstasy. The clasp of the miniature stays around her small body was like the embrace of a little lover, and awoke in her ideas that were as vague, as immature and unformed as the straight little figure itself.

When Snooky and Howard had seated themselves, but one chair—at the end of the breakfast-table, opposite Mr. Bessemer—remained vacant.

"Is your sister—is Miss Travis going to have her breakfast now? Is she got up yet?" inquired Victorine of Howard and Snooky, as she pushed the cream pitcher out of Howard's reach. It was significant of Mr. Bessemer's relations with his family that Victorine did not address her question to him.

"Yes, yes, she's coming," said both the children, speaking together; and Howard added: "Here she comes now."

Travis Bessemer came in. Even in San Francisco, where all women are more or less beautiful, Travis passed for a beautiful girl. She was young, but tall as most men, and solidly, almost heavily built. Her shoulders were broad, her chest was deep, her neck round and firm. She radiated health; there were exuberance and vitality in the very touch of her foot upon the carpet, and there was that cleanliness about her, that freshness, that suggested a recent plunge in the surf and a "constitutional" along the beach. One felt that here was stamina, good physical force, and fine animal vigor. Her arms were large, her wrists were large, and her fingers did not taper. Her hair was of a brown so light as to be almost yellow. In fact, it would be safer to call it yellow from the start—not golden nor flaxen, but plain, honest yellow. The skin of her face was clean and white, except where it flushed to a most charming pink upon her smooth, cool cheeks. Her lips were full and red, her chin very round and a little salient. Curiously enough, her eyes were small—small, but of the deepest, deepest brown, and always twinkling and alight, as though she were just ready to smile or had just done smiling, one could not say which. And nothing could have been more delightful than these sloe-brown, glinting little eyes of hers set off by her white skin and yellow hair.

She impressed one as being a very normal girl: nothing morbid about her, nothing nervous or false or overwrought. You did not expect to find her introspective. You felt sure that her mental life was not at all the result of thoughts and reflections germinating from within, but rather of impressions and sensations that came to her from without. There was nothing extraordinary about Travis. She never had her vagaries, was not moody—depressed one day and exalted the next. She was just a good, sweet, natural, healthy-minded, healthy-bodied girl, honest, strong, self-reliant, and good-tempered.

Though she was not yet dressed for church, there was style in her to the pointed tips of her patent-leather slippers. She wore a heavy black overskirt that rustled in delicious fashion over the colored silk skirt beneath, and a white shirt-waist, striped black, and starched to a rattling stiffness. Her neck was swathed tight and high with a broad ribbon of white satin, while around her waist, in place of a belt, she wore the huge dog-collar of a St. Bernard—a chic little idea which was all her own, and of which she was very proud.

She was as trig and trim and crisp as a crack yacht: not a pin was loose, not a seam that did not fall in its precise right line; and with every movement there emanated from her a barely perceptible delicious feminine odor—an odor that was in part perfume, but mostly a subtle, vague smell, charming beyond words, that came from her hair, her neck, her arms—her whole sweet personality. She was nineteen years old.

She sat down to breakfast and ate heartily, though with her attention divided between Howard—who was atrociously bad, as usual of a Sunday morning—and her father's plate. Mr. Bessemer was as like as not to leave the table without any breakfast at all unless his fruit, chops, and coffee were actually thrust under his nose.

"Papum," she called, speaking clear and distinct, as though to the deaf, "there's your coffee there at your elbow; be careful, you'll tip it over. Victorine, push his cup further on the table. Is it strong enough for you, Papum?"

"Eh? Ah, yes—yes—yes," murmured the old man, looking vaguely about him; "coffee, to be sure"—and he emptied the cup at a single draught, hardly knowing whether it was coffee or tea. "Now I'll take a roll," he continued, in a monotonous murmur. "Where are the rolls? Here they are. Hot rolls are bad for my digestion—I ought to eat bread. I think I eat too much. Where's my place in the paper?—always lose my place in the paper. Clever editorials this fellow Eastman writes, unbiased by party prejudice—unbiased—unbiased." His voice died to a whisper.

The breakfast proceeded, Travis supervising everything that went forward, even giving directions to Victorine as to the hour for serving dinner. It was while she was talking to Victorine as to this matter that Snooky began to whine, "Stop!"

"And tell Maggie," pursued Travis, "to fricassee her chicken, and not to have it too well done—"

"*Sto-o-op!*" whined Snooky again.

"And leave the heart out for Papum. He likes the heart—"

"Sto-o-op!"

"Unbiased by prejudice," murmured Mr. Bessemer, "vigorous and to the point. I'll have another roll."

"Pa, make Howard stop!"

"Howard!" exclaimed Travis; "what is it now?"

"Howard's squirting watermelon seeds at me," whined Snooky, "and Pa won't make him stop."

"Oh, I didn't so!" vociferated Howard. "I only held one between my fingers, and it just kind of shot out."

"You'll come upstairs with me in just five minutes," announced Travis, "and get ready for Sunday-school."

Howard knew that his older sister's decisions were as the laws of the Persians, and found means to finish his breakfast within the specified time, though not without protest. Once upstairs, however, the usual Sunday morning drama of despatching him to Sunday-school in presentable condition was enacted. At every moment his voice could be heard uplifted in shrill expostulation and debate. No, his hands were clean enough, and he didn't see why he had to wear that little old pink tie; and, oh! His new shoes were too tight and hurt his sore toe; and he wouldn't, he wouldn't—no, not if he were killed for it, change his shirt. Not for a moment did Travis lose her temper with him. But "very well," she declared at length, "the next time she saw that little Miner girl she would tell her that he had said she was his beau-heart. *Now* would he hold still while she brushed his hair?"

At a few minutes before eleven Travis and her father went to church. They were Episcopalians, and for time out of mind had rented a half-pew in the church of their denomination on California Street, not far from Chinatown. By noon the family reassembled. at dinner-table, where Mr. Bessemer ate his chicken-heart—after Travis had thrice reminded him of it—and expressed himself as to the sermon and the minister's theology: sometimes to his daughter and sometimes to himself.

After dinner Howard and Snooky foregathered in the nursery with their beloved lead soldiers; Travis went to her room to write letters; and Mr. Bessemer sat in the bay window of the dining-room reading the paper from end to end.

At five Travis bestirred herself. It was Victorine's afternoon out. Travis set the table, spreading a cover of blue denim edged with white braid, which showed off the silver and the set of delft—her great and never-ending joy—to great effect. Then she tied her apron about her, and went into the kitchen to make the mayonnaise dressing for the potato salad, to slice the ham, and to help the cook (a most inefficient Irish person, taken on only for that month during the absence of the family's beloved and venerated Sing Wo) in the matter of preparing the Sunday evening tea.

Tea was had at half-past five. Never in the history of the family had its menu varied: cold ham, potato salad, pork and beans, canned fruit, chocolate, and the inevitable pitcher of ice-water.

In the absence of Victorine, Maggie waited on the table, very uncomfortable in her one good dress and stiff white apron. She stood off from the table, making awkward dabs at it from time to time. In her excess of deference she developed a clumsiness that was beyond all expression. She passed the plates upon the wrong side, and remembered herself with a broken apology at inopportune moments. She dropped a spoon, she spilled the ice-water. She handled the delft cups and platters with an exaggerated solicitude, as though they were glass bombs. She brushed the crumbs into their laps instead of into the crumb-tray, and at last, when she had sat even

Travis' placid nerves in a jangle, was dismissed to the kitchen, and retired with a gasp of unspeakable relief.

Suddenly there came a prolonged trilling of the electric bell, and Howard flashed a grin at Travis. Snooky jumped up and pushed back, crying out: "I'll go! I'll go!"

Mr. Bessemer glanced nervously at Travis. "That's Mr. Rivers, isn't it, daughter?" Travis smiled. "Well, I think I'll—I think I'd better—" he began.

"No," said Travis, "I don't want you to, Papum; you sit right where you are. How absurd!"

The old man dropped obediently back into his seat.

"That's all right, Maggie," said Travis as the cook reappeared from the pantry. "Snooky went."

"Huh!" exclaimed Howard, his grin widening. "Huh!"

"And remember one thing, Howard," remarked Travis calmly, "don't you ever again ask Mr. Rivers for a nickel to put in your bank."

Mr. Bessemer roused up. "Did that boy do that?" he inquired sharply of Travis.

"Well, well, he won't do it again," said Travis soothingly. The old man glared for an instant at Howard, who shifted uneasily in his seat. But meanwhile Snooky had clambered down to the outside door, and before anything further could be said young Rivers came into the dining-room.

Chapter II

FOR some reason, never made sufficiently clear, Rivers' parents had handicapped him from the baptismal font with the prenomen of Conde, which, however, upon Anglo-Saxon tongues, had been promptly modified to Condy, or even, among his familiar and intimate friends, to Conny. Asked as to his birthplace—for no Californian assumes that his neighbor is born in the State—Condy was wont to reply that he was "bawn 'n' rais'" in Chicago; "but," he always added, "I couldn't help that, you know." His people had come West in the early eighties, just in time to bury the father in alien soil. Condy was an only child. He was educated at the State University, had a finishing year at Yale, and a few months after his return home was taken on the staff of the San Francisco *Daily Times* as an associate editor of its Sunday supplement. For Condy had developed a taste and talent in the matter of writing. Short stories were his mania. He had begun by an inoculation of the Kipling virus, had suffered an almost fatal attack of Harding Davis, and had even been affected by Maupassant. He "went in" for accuracy of detail; held that if one wrote a story involving firemen one should have, or seem to have, every detail of the department at his fingers' ends, and should "bring in" to the tale all manner of technical names and cant phrases.

Much of his work on the Sunday supplement of *The Times* was of the hack order—special articles, writeups, and interviews. About once a month, however, he wrote a short story, and of late, now that he was convalescing from Maupassant and had begun to be somewhat himself, these stories had improved in quality, and one or two had even been copied in the Eastern journals. He earned $100 a month.

When Snooky had let him in, Rivers dashed up the stairs of the Bessemers' flat, two at a time, tossed his stick into a porcelain cane-rack in the hall, wrenched off his overcoat with a single movement, and precipitated himself, panting, into the dining-room, tugging at his gloves.

He was twenty-eight years old—nearly ten years older than Travis; tall and somewhat lean; his face smooth-shaven and pink all over, as if he had just given it a violent rubbing with a crash towel. Unlike most writing folk, he dressed himself according to prevailing custom. But Condy overdid the matter. His scarfs and cravats were too bright, his colored shirt-bosoms were too broadly barred, his waistcoats too extreme. Even Travis, as she rose to his abrupt entrance? told herself that of a Sunday evening a pink shirt and scarlet tie were a combination hardly to be forgiven.

Condy shook her hand in both of his, then rushed over to Mr. Bessemer, exclaiming between breaths: "Don't get up, sir—don't *think* of it! Heavens! I'm disgustingly late. You're all through. My watch—this beastly watch of mine—I can't imagine how I came to be so late. You did quite right not to wait."

Then as his morbidly keen observation caught a certain look of blankness on Travis' face, and his rapid glance noted no vacant chair at table, he gave a quick gasp of dismay.

"Heavens and earth! Didn't you *expect* me?" he cried. "I thought you said—I thought—I must have forgotten—I must have got it mixed up somehow. What a hideous mistake, what a blunder! What a fool I am!"

He dropped into a chair against the wall and mopped his forehead with a blue-bordered handkerchief.

"Well, what difference does it make, Condy?" said Travis quietly. "I'll put another place for you."

"No, no!" he vociferated, jumping up. "I won't hear of it, I won't permit it! You'll think I did it on purpose!"

Travis ignored his interference, and made a place for him opposite the children, and had Maggie make some more chocolate.

Condy meanwhile covered himself with opprobrium.

"And all this trouble—I always make trouble everywhere I go. Always a round man in a square hole, or a square man in a round hole."

He got up and sat down again, crossed and recrossed his legs, picked up little ornaments from the mantelpiece, and replaced them without consciousness of what they were, and finally broke the crystal of his watch as he was resetting it by the cuckoo clock.

"Hello!" he exclaimed suddenly, "where did you get that clock? Where did you get that clock? That's new to me. Where did that come from?"

"That cuckoo clock?" inquired Travis, with a stare. "Condy Rivers, you've been here and in this room at least twice a week for the last year and a half, and that clock, and no other, has always hung there."

But already Condy had forgotten or lost interest in the clock.

"Is that so? is that so?" he murmured absent-mindedly, seating himself at the table.

Mr. Bessemer was murmuring: "That clock's a little fast. I can not make that clock keep time. Victorine has lost the key. I have to wind it with a monkey-wrench. Now I'll try some more beans. Maggie has put in too much pepper. I'll have to have a new key made tomorrow."

"Hey? Yes—yes. Is that so?" answered Condy Rivers, bewildered, wishing to be polite, yet unable to follow the old man's mutterings.

"He's not talking to you," remarked Travis, without lowering her voice. "You know how Papum goes on. He won't hear a word you say. Well, I read your story in this morning's *Times*."

A few moments later, while Travers and Condy were still discussing this story, Mr. Bessemer rose. "Well, Mr. Rivers," he announced, "I guess I'll say good-night. Come, Snooky."

"Yes, take her with you, Papum," said Travis. "She'll go to sleep on the lounge here if you don't. Howard, have you got your lessons for tomorrow?"

It appeared that he had not. Snooky whined to stay up a little longer, but at last consented to go with her father. They all bade Condy good-night and took themselves away, Howard lingering a moment in the door in the hope of the nickel he dared not ask for. Maggie reappeared to clear away the table.

"Let's go in the parlor," suggested Travis, rising. "Don't you want to?"

The parlor was the front room overlooking the street, and was reached by the long hall that ran the whole length of the flat, passing by the door of each one of its eight rooms in turn.

Travis preceded Condy, and turned up one of the burners in colored globe of the little brass chandelier.

The parlor was a small affair, peopled by a family of chairs and sofas robed in white drugget. A gold-and-white effect had been striven for throughout the room. The walls had been tinted instead of papered, and bunches of hand-painted pink flowers tied up with blue ribbons straggled from one corner of the ceiling. Across one angle of the room straddled a brass easel upholding a crayon portrait of Travis at the age of nine, "enlarged from a photograph." A yellow drape ornamented one corner of the frame, while another drape of blue depended from one end of the mantelpiece.

The piano, upon which nobody ever played, balanced the easel in an opposite corner. Over the mantelpiece hung in a gilded frame a steel engraving of Priscilla and John Alden; and on the mantel itself two bisque figures of an Italian fisher boy and girl kept company with the clock, a huge timepiece, set in a red plush palette, that never was known to go. But at the right of the fireplace, and balancing the tuft of pampa-grass to the left, was an inverted section of a sewer-pipe painted blue and decorated with daisies. Into it was thrust a sheaf of cattails, gilded, and tied with a pink ribbon.

Travis dropped upon the shrouded sofa, and Condy set himself carefully down on one of the frail chairs with its spindling golden legs, and they began to talk.

Condy had taken her to the theater the Monday night of that week, as had been his custom ever since he had known her well, and there was something left for them to say on that subject. But in ten minutes they had exhausted it. An engagement of a girl known to both of them had just been announced. Condy brought that up, and kept conversation going for another twenty minutes, and then filled in what threatened to be a gap by telling her stories of the society reporters, and how they got inside news by listening to telephone party wires for days at a time. Travis' condemnation of this occupied another five or ten minutes; and so what with this and with that they reached nine o'clock. Then decidedly the evening began to drag. It was too early to go. Condy could find no good excuse for taking himself away, and, though Travis was good-natured enough, and met him more than halfway, their talk lapsed, and lapsed, and lapsed. The breaks became more numerous and lasted longer. Condy began to wonder if he was boring her. No sooner had the suspicion entered his head than it hardened into a certainty, and at once what little fluency and freshness he yet retained forsook him on the spot. What made matters worse was his recollection of other evenings that of late he had failed in precisely the same manner. Even while he struggled to save the situation Condy was wondering if they two were talked out—if they had lost charm for each other. Did he not know Travis through and through by now—her opinions, her ideas, her convictions? Was there any more freshness in her for him? Was their little flirtation of the last eighteen months, charming as it had been, about to end? Had they played out the play, had they come to the end of each other's resources? He had never considered the possibility of this before, but all at once as he looked at Travis—looked fairly into her little brown-black eyes—it was borne in upon him that she was thinking precisely the same thing.

Condy Rivers had met Travis at a dance a year and a half before this, and, because she was so very pretty, so unaffected, and so good-natured, had found means to see her three or four times a week ever since. They two "went out" not a little in San Francisco society, and had been in a measure identified with what was known as the Younger Set; though Travis was too young to come out, and Rivers too old to feel very much at home with girls of twenty and boys of eighteen.

They had known each other in the conventional way (as convention-

ality goes in San Francisco); during the season Rivers took her to the theaters Monday nights, and called regularly Wednesdays and Sundays. Then
they met at dances, and managed to be invited to the same houses for teas
and dinners. They had flirted rather desperately, and at times Condy even
told himself that he loved this girl so much younger than he—this girl with
the smiling eyes and robust figure and yellow hair, who was so frank, so
straightforward, and so wonderfully pretty.

But evidently they had come to the last move in the game, and as
Condy reflected that after all he had never known the real Travis, that the
girl whom he told himself he knew through and through was only the
Travis of dinner parties and afternoon functions, he was suddenly surprised to experience a sudden qualm of deep and genuine regret. He had
never been *near* to her, after all. They were as far apart as when they had
first met. And yet he knew enough of her to know that she was "worth
while." He had had experience—all the experience he wanted—with other
older women and girls of society. They were sophisticated, they were all a
little tired, they had run the gamut of amusements—in a word, they were
jaded. But Travis, this girl of nineteen, who was not yet even a debutante,
had been fresh and unspoiled, had been new and strong and young.

"Of course, you may call it what you like. He was nothing more nor
less than intoxicated—yes, drunk."

"Hah! Who—what—wh—what are you talking about?" gasped Condy
sitting bolt upright.

"Jack Carter," answered Travis. "No," she added. shaking her head at
him helplessly, "he hasn't been listening to a word. I'm talking about Jack
Carter and the 'Saturday Evening' last night."

"No, no, I haven't heard. Forgive me; I was thinking—thinking of
something else. Who was drunk?"

Travis paused a moment, settling her side-combs in her hair; then:

"If you will try to listen, I'll tell it all over again, because it's serious
with me, and I'm going to take a very decided stand about it. You know,"
she went on, "you know what the 'Saturday Evening' is. Plenty of the girls
who are not 'out' belong, and a good many of last year's debutantes come,
as well as the older girls of three or four seasons' standing. You could call it
representative couldn't you? Well, they always serve punch; and you know
yourself that you have seen men there who have taken more than they
should."

"Yes, yes," admitted Condy. "I know Carter and the two Catlin boys
always do."

"It gets pretty bad sometimes, doesn't it?" she said.

"It does, it does—and it's shameful. But most of the girls—*most* of them don't seem to mind."

Miss Bessemer stiffened a bit. "There are one or two girls that do," she said quietly. "Frank Catlin had the decency to go home last night," she continued; "and his brother wasn't any worse than usual. But Jack Carter must have been drinking before he came. He was very bad indeed—as bad," she said between her teeth, "as he could be and yet walk straight. As you say, most of the girls don't mind. They say, 'It's only Johnnie Carter; what do you expect?' But one of the girls—you know her, Laurie Flagg—cut a dance with him last night and told him exactly why. Of course, Carter was furious. He was sober enough to think he had been insulted; and what do you suppose he did?"

"What? what?" exclaimed Condy, breathless, leaning toward her.

"Went about the halls and dressing-rooms circulating some dirty little lie about Laurie. Actually trying to—to"—Travis hesitated—"to make a scandal about her."

Condy bounded in his seat. "Beast, cad, swine!" he exclaimed.

"I didn't think," said Travis, "that Carter would so much as dare to ask me to dance with him—"

"Did he? did—did—"

"Wait," she interrupted. "So I wasn't at all prepared for what happened. Before I knew it, there he was in front of me. It was a break, and he wanted it. I hadn't time to think. The only idea I had was that if I refused him he might tell some dirty little lie about me. I was all confused—mixed up. I felt just as though it were a snake that I had to humor to get rid of. I gave him the break."

Condy sat speechless. Suddenly he arose.

"Well, now, let's see," he began, speaking rapidly, his hands twisting and untwisting till the knuckles cracked. "Now, let's see. You leave it to me. I know Carter. He's going to be at a stag dinner where I am invited tomorrow night, and I—I—"

"No, you won't, Condy," said Travis placidly. "You'll pay no attention to it, and I'll tell you why. Suppose you should make a scene with Mr. Carter—I don't know how men settle these things. Well, it would be told in all the clubs and in all the newspaper offices that two men had quarreled over a girl; and my name is mentioned, discussed, and handed around from one crowd of men to another, from one club to another; and then, of course, the papers take it up. By that time Mr. Carter will have told his side of the story and invented another dirty little lie, and I'm the one who suffers the most in the end. And remember, Condy, that I haven't any mother in such an affair, not even an older sister. No, we'll just let the matter drop. It would be more dignified, anyhow. Only I have made up my mind what I am going to do."

"What's that?"

"I'm not coming out. If that's the sort of thing one has to put up with in society"—Travis drew a little line on the sofa at her side with her fingertip—"I am going to—stop—right—there. It's not"—Miss Bessemer stiffened again—"that I'm afraid of Jack Carter and his dirty stories; I simply don't want to know the kind of people who have made Jack Carter possible. The other girls don't mind it, nor many men besides you, Condy; and I'm not going to be associated with people who take it as a joke for a man to come to a function drunk. And as for having a good time, I'll find my amusements somewhere else. I'll ride a wheel, take long walks, study something. But as for leading the life of a society girl—no! And whether I have a good time or not, I'll keep my own self-respect. At least I'll never have to dance with a drunken man. I won't have to humiliate myself like that a second time."

"But I presume you will still continue to go out somewhere," protested Condy Rivers.

She shook her head.

"I have thought it all over, and I've talked about it with Papum. There's no half way about it. The only way to stop is to stop short. Just this afternoon I've regretted three functions for next week, and I shall resign from the 'Saturday Evening.' Oh, it's not the Jack Carter affair alone!" she exclaimed; "the whole thing tires me. Mind, Condy," she exclaimed, "I'm not going to break with it because I have any 'purpose in life,' or that sort of thing. I want to have a good time, and I'm going to see if I can't have it in my own way. If the kind of thing that makes Jack Carter possible is conventionality, then I'm done with conventionality for good. I am going to try, from this time on, to be just as true to myself as I can be. I am going to be sincere, and not pretend to like people and things that I don't like; and I'm going to do the things that I like to do—just so long as they are the things a good girl can do. See, Condy?"

"You're fine," murmured Condy breathless. "You're fine as gold, Travis, and I—I love you all the better for it."

"Ah, *now!*" exclaimed Travis, with a brusque movement, "there's mother thing we must talk about. No more foolishness between us. We've had a jolly little flirtation, I know, and it's been good fun while it lasted. I know you like me, and you know that I like you; but as for loving each other, you know we don't. Yes, you say that you love me and that I'm the only girl. That's part of the game. I can play it"—her little eyes began to dance—"quite as well as you. But it's playing with something that's quite too serious to be played with—after all, isn't it, now? It's insincere, and, as I tell you, from now on I'm going to be as true and as sincere and as honest as I can."

"But I tell you that I *do* love you," protested Condy, trying to make the words ring true.

Travis looked about the room an instant as if in deliberation; then abruptly: "Ah! What am I going to *do* with such a boy as you are, after all—a great big, overgrown boy? Condy Rivers, look at me straight in the eye. Tell me, do you honestly love me? You know what I mean when I say 'love.' Do you love me?"

"No, I don't!" he exclaimed blankly, as though he had just discovered the fact.

"There!" declared Travis—"and I don't love you."

They both began to laugh.

"Now," added Travis, "we don't need to have the burden and trouble of keeping up the pretenses any more. We understand each other, don't we?"

"This is queer enough," said Condy drolly.

"But isn't it an improvement?"

Condy scoured his head.

"Tell me the truth," she insisted. "*You* be sincere."

"I do believe it is. Why—why—Travis by Jingo! Travis, I think I'm going to like you better than ever now."

"Never mind. Is it an agreement?"

"What is?"

"That we don't pretend to love each other any more?"

"All right—yes—you're right; because the moment I began to love you I should like you so much less."

She put out her hand. "That's an agreement, then."

Condy took her hand in his. "Yes, it's an agreement." But when, as had been his custom, he made as though to kiss her hand, Travis drew it quickly away.

"No! No!" she said firmly, smiling for all that. "No more foolishness."

"But—but," he protested, "it's not so radical as that, is it? You're not going to overturn such time-worn, time-honored customs as that? Why, this is a regular rebellion."

"No, sire," quoted Travis, trying not to laugh, "it is a revolution."

Chapter III

Although Monday was practically a holiday for the Sunday-supplement staff of *The Times*, Condy Rivers made a point to get down to the office betimes the next morning. There were reasons why a certain article descriptive of a great whaleback steamer taking on grain for famine-stricken India should be written that day, and Rivers wanted his afternoon free in order to go to Laurie Flagg's coming-out tea.

But as he came into his room at *The Times* office, which he shared with the exchange and sporting editors, and settled himself at his desk, he suddenly remembered that, under the new order of things, he need not expect to see Travis at the Flaggs'.

"Well," he muttered, "maybe it doesn't make so much difference, after all. She was a corking fine girl, but—might as well admit it—the play is played out. Of course, I don't love her—any more than she loves me. I'll see less and less of her now. It's inevitable, and after a while we'll hardly even meet. In a way, it's a pity; but, of course, one has to be sensible about these things. . . . Well, this whaleback now."

He rang up the Chamber of Commerce, and found out that the "City of Everett," which was the whaleback's name, was at the Mission Street wharf. This made it possible for him to write the article in two ways. He either could fake his copy from a clipping on the subject which the exchange editor had laid on his desk, or he could go down in person to the wharf, interview the captain, and inspect the craft for himself. The former was the short and easy method. The latter was more troublesome, but would result in a far more interesting article.

Condy debated the subject a few minutes, then decided to go down to the wharf. San Francisco's waterfront was always interesting, and he might get hold of a photograph of the whaleback. All at once the "idea" of the article struck him, the certain underlying notion that would give importance and weight to the mere details and descriptions. Condy's enthusiasm flared up in an instant.

"By Jove!" he exclaimed; "by Jove!"

He clapped on his hat wrong side foremost, crammed a sheaf of copy-paper into his pocket, and was on the street again in another moment. Then it occurred to him that he had forgotten to call at his club that morning for his mail, as was his custom, on the way to the office. He looked at his watch. It was early yet, and his club was but two blocks' distance. He decided that he would get his letters at the club, and read them on the way down to the wharf.

For Condy had joined a certain San Francisco club of artists, journalists, musicians, and professional men that is one of the institutions of the city, and, in fact, famous throughout the United States. He was one of the younger members, but was popular and well liked, and on more than one occasion had materially contributed to the fun of the club's "low jinks."

In his box this morning he found one letter that he told himself he must read upon the instant. It bore upon the envelope the name of a New York publishing house to whom Condy had sent a collection of his short stories about a month before. He took the letter into the "round window" of the club, overlooking the street, and tore it open excitedly. The fact that he had received a letter from the firm without the return of his manuscript seemed a good omen. This was what he read:

Conde Rivers, Esq.,
Bohemian Club, San Francisco, Cal.

DEAR SIR:
    We return to you by this mail the manuscript of your stories, which we do not consider as available for publication at the present moment. We would say, however, that we find in several of them indications of a quite unusual order of merit. The best-selling book just now is the short novel—say thirty thousand words—of action and adventure. Judging from the stories of your collection, we suspect that your talent lies in this direction, and we would suggest that you write such a novel and submit the same to us.
    Very respectfully,
                            THE CENTENNIAL CO.,
                            New York.

Condy shoved the letter into his pocket and collapsed limply into his chair.

"What's the good of trying to do anything anyhow!" he muttered, looking gloomily down into the street. "My level is just the hack-work of a local Sunday supplement, and I am a fool to think of anything else."

His enthusiasm in the matter of the "City of Everett" was cold and dead in a moment. He could see no possibilities in the subject whatever. His "idea" of a few minutes previous seemed ridiculous and overwrought. He would go back to the office and grind out his copy from the exchange editor's clipping.

Just then his eye was caught by a familiar figure in trim, well-fitting black halted on the opposite corner waiting for the passage of a cable car. It was Travis Bessemer. No one but she could carry off such rigorous simplicity in the matter of dress so well: black skirt, black Russian blouse, tiny black bonnet and black veil, white kids with black stitching. Simplicity itself. Yet the style of her, as Condy Rivers told himself, flew up and hit you in the face; and her figure—was there anything more perfect? and the soft pretty effect of her yellow hair seen through the veil—could anything be more fetching? and her smart carriage and the fling of her fine broad shoulders, and—no, it was no use; Condy had to run down to speak to her.

"Come, come!" she said as he pretended to jostle against her on the curbstone without noticing her; "you had best go to work. Loafing at ten o'clock on the street corners—the idea!"

"It *is* not—it can not be—and yet it is—it is *she*," he burlesqued; "and after all these years!" Then in his natural voice: "Hello T.B."

"Hello, C.R."

"Where are you going?"

"Home. I've just run down for half an hour to have the head of my banjo tightened."

"If I put you on the car, will you expect me to pay your car-fare?"

"Condy Rivers, I've long since got over the idea of ever expecting you to have any change concealed about your person."

"Huh! No, it all goes for theater tickets, and flowers, and boxes of candy for a certain girl I know. But"—and he glared at her significantly—"no more foolishness."

She laughed. "What are you 'on' this morning, Condy?"

Condy told her as they started to walk toward Kearney Street.

"But why *don't* you go to the dock and see the vessel, if you can make a better article that way?"

"Oh, what's the good! The Centennial people have turned down my stories."

She commiserated him for this; then suddenly exclaimed:

"No, you must go down to the dock! You ought to, Condy Oh, I tell you, let me go down with you!"

In an instant Condy leaped to the notion. "Splendid! Splendid! No reason why you shouldn't!" he exclaimed. And within fifteen minutes the two were treading the wharves and quays of the city's waterfront.

Ships innumerable nuzzled at the endless line of docks, mast overspiring mast, and bowsprit overlapping bowsprit, till the eye was bewildered, as if by the confusion of branches in a leafless forest. In the distance the mass of rigging resolved itself into a solid gray blur against the sky. The great hulks, green and black and slate gray, laid themselves along the docks, straining leisurely at their mammoth chains, their flanks opened, their cargoes, as it were their entrails, spewed out in a wild disarray of crate and bale and box. Sailors and stevedores swarmed them like vermin. Trucks rolled along the wharves like peals of ordnance, the horse-hoofs beating the boards like heavy drum-taps. Chains clanked, a ship's dog barked incessantly from a companionway, ropes creaked in complaining pulleys, blocks rattled, hoisting-engines coughed and strangled, while all the air was redolent of oakum, of pitch, of paint, of spices, of ripe fruit, of clean cool lumber, of coffee, of tar, of bilge, and the brisk, nimble odor of the sea.

Travis was delighted, her little brown eyes snapping, her cheeks flushing, as she drank in the scene.

"To think," she cried, "where all these ships have come from! Look at their names; aren't they perfect? Just the names, see: the *Mary Baker*, Hull; and the *Anandale*, Liverpool; and the *Two Sisters*, Calcutta, and see that one they're calking, the *Montevideo*, Callao; and there, look! Look! The very one you're looking for, the *City of Everett*, San Francisco."

The whaleback, an immense tube of steel plates, lay at her wharf, sucking in entire harvests of wheat from the San Joaquin valley—harvests that were to feed strangely clad skeletons on the southern slopes of the Himalaya foothills. Travis and Condy edged their way among piles of wheat-bags, dodging drays and rumbling trucks, and finally brought up at the after gangplank, where a sailor halted them. Condy exhibited his reporter's badge.

"I represent *The Times*," he said, with profound solemnity, "and I want to see the officer in charge."

The sailor fell back upon the instant.

"Power of the press," whispered Condy to Travis as the two gained the deck.

A second sailor directed them to the mate, whom they found in the chart-room, engaged, singularly enough, in trimming the leaves of a scraggly geranium.

Condy explained his mission with flattering allusions to the whaleback and the novelty of the construction. The mate—an old man with a patriarchal beard—softened at once, asked them into his own cabin aft, and even brought out a camp-stool for Travis, brushing it with his sleeve before setting it down.

While Condy was interviewing the old fellow, Travis was examining, with the interest of a child, the details of the cabin: the rack-like bunk, the washstand, ingeniously constructed so as to shut into the bulkhead when not in use, the alarm-clock screwed to the wall, and the array of photographs thrust into the mirror between frame and glass. One, an old daguerreotype, particularly caught her fancy. It was the portrait of a very beautiful girl, wearing the old-fashioned side curls and high comb of a half-century previous. The old mate noticed the attention she paid to it, and, as soon as he had done giving information to Condy, turned and nodded to Travis, and said quietly: "She was pretty, wasn't she?"

"Oh, very!" answered Travis, without looking away.

There was a silence. Then the mate, his eyes wide and thoughtful, said with a long breath:

"And she was just about your age, miss, when I saw her; and you favor her, too."

Condy and Travis held their breaths in attention. There in the cabin of that curious nondescript whaleback they had come suddenly to the edge of a romance—a romance that had been lived through before they were born. Then Travis said in a low voice, and sweetly:

"She died?"

"Before I ever set eyes on her, miss. That is, *maybe* she died. I sometimes think—fact is, I really believe she's alive yet, and waiting for me." He hesitated awkwardly. "I dunno," he said pulling his beard. "I don't usually tell that story to strange folk, but you remind me so of her that I guess I will."

Condy sat down on the edge of the bunk, and the mate seated himself on the plush settle opposite the door, his elbows on his knees, his eyes fixed on a patch of bright sunlight upon the deck outside.

"I began life," he said, "as a deep-sea diver—began pretty young, too. I first put on the armor when I was twenty, nothing but a lad; but I could take the pressure up to seventy pounds even then. One of my very first dives was off Trincomalee, on the coast of Ceylon. A mail packet had gone down in a squall with all on board. Six of the bodies had come up and had been recovered, but the seventh hadn't. It was the body of the daughter of the governor of the island, a beautiful young girl of nineteen, whom everybody loved. I was sent for to go down and bring the body up. Well, I went down. The packet lay in a hundred feet of water, and that's a wonder deep dive. I had to go down twice. The first time I couldn't find anything, though I went all through the berth-deck. I came up to the wrecking-float and reported that I had seen nothing. There were a lot of men there belonging to the wrecking gang, and some correspondents of London papers. But they would have it that she was below, and had me go down again. I did, and this time I found her."

The mate paused a moment.

"I'll have to tell you," he went on, "that when a body don't come to the surface it will stand or sit in a perfectly natural position until a current or movement of the water around touches it. When that happens—well, you'd say the body was alive; and old divers have a superstition—no, it *ain't* just a superstition, I believe it's so—that drowned people really don't die till they come to the surface, and the air touches them. We say that the drowned who don't come up still have some sort of life of their own way down there in all that green water . . . some kind of life . . . surely . . . surely. When I went down the second time, I came across the door of what I thought at first was the linen-closet. But it turned out to be a little state-room. I opened it. There was the girl. She was sitting on the sofa opposite the door, with a little hat on her head, and holding a satchel in her lap, just as if she was ready to go ashore. Her eyes were wide open, and she was looking right at me and smiling. It didn't seem terrible or ghastly in the least. She seemed very sweet. When I opened the door it set the water in motion, and she got up and dropped the satchel, and came toward me smiling and holding out her arms.

"I stepped back quick and shut the door, and sat down in one of the saloon chairs to fetch my breath, for it had given me a start. The next thing to do was to send her up. But I began to think. She seemed so pretty as she was. What was the use of bringing her up—up there on the wrecking float with that crowd of men—up where the air would get at her, and where they would put her in the ground along o' the worms? If I left her there she'd always be sweet and pretty—always be nineteen; and I remembered what old divers said about drowned people living just so long as they stayed below. You see, I was only a lad then, and things like that impress you when you're young. Well, I signaled to be hauled up. They asked me on the float if I'd seen anything, and I said no. That was all there was to the affair. They never raised the ship, and in a little while it was all forgotten.

"But I never forgot it, and I always remembered her, way down there in all that still green water, waiting there in that little state-room for me to come back and open the door. And I've growed to be an old man remembering her; but she's always stayed just as she was the first day I saw her, when she came toward me smiling and holding out her arms. She's always stayed young and fresh and pretty. I never saw her but that once. Only afterward I got her picture from a native woman of Trincomalee who was housekeeper at the Residency where the governor of the island lived. Somehow I never could care for other women after that, and I ain't never married for that reason."

"No, no, of course not!" exclaimed Travis, in a low voice as the old fellow paused.

"Fine, fine; oh, fine as gold!" murmured Condy, under his breath.

"Well," said the mate, getting up and rubbing his knee, "that's the story. Now you know all about that picture. Will you have a glass of Madeira, miss?"

He got out a bottle of wine bearing the genuine Funchal label and filled three tiny glasses. Travis pushed up her veil, and she and Condy rose.

"This is to *her*," said Travis gravely.

"Thank you, miss," answered the mate, and the three drank in silence.

As Travis and Condy were going down the gangplank they met the captain of the whaleback coming up.

"I saw you in there talking to old McPherson," he explained. "Did you get what you wanted from him?"

"More, more!" exclaimed Condy.

"My hand in the fire, he told you that yarn about the girl who was drowned off Trincomalee. Of course, I knew it. The old boy's wits are turned on that subject. He will have it that the body hasn't decomposed in all this time. Good seaman enough, and a first-class navigator, but he's soft in that one spot."

Chapter IV

"Oh, but the *story* of it!" exclaimed Condy as he and Travis regained the wharf—"the story of it! Isn't it a ripper. Isn't it a corker! His leaving her that way, and never caring for any other girl afterward."

"And so original," she commented, quite as enthusiastic as he.

"Original?—why, it's new as paint! It's—it's—Travis, I'll make a story out of this that will be copied in every paper between the two oceans."

They were so interested in the mate's story that they forgot to take a car, and walked up Clay Street talking it over, suggesting, rearranging, and embellishing; and Condy was astonished and delighted to note that she "caught on" to the idea as quickly as he, and knew the telling points and what details to leave out.

"And I'll make a bang-up article out of the whaleback herself," declared Condy. The "idea" of the article had returned to him, and all his enthusiasm with it.

"And look here," he said, showing her the letter from the Centennial Company. "They turned down my book, but see what they say."

"Quite an unusual order of merit!" cried Travis. "Why, that's fine! Why didn't you show this to me before?—and asking you like this to write them a novel of adventure! What *more* can you want? Oh!" she exclaimed impatiently, "that's so like you; you would tell everybody about your reverses, and carry on about them yourself, but never say a word when you get a little boom. Have you an idea for a thirty-thousand-word novel? Wouldn't that diver's story do?"

"No, there's not enough in that for thirty thousand words. I haven't any idea at all—never wrote a story of adventure—never wrote anything longer than six thousand words. But I'll keep my eye open for something that will do. By the way—by Jove! Travis, where are we?"

They looked briskly around them, and the bustling, breezy waterfront faded from their recollections. They were in a world of narrow streets, of galleries and overhanging balconies. Craziest structures, riddled and honeycombed with stairways and passages, shut out the sky, though here and there rose a building of extraordinary richness and most elaborate ornamentation. Color was everywhere. A thousand little notes of green and yellow, of vermilion and sky blue, assaulted the eye. Here it was a doorway, here a vivid glint of cloth or hanging, here a huge scarlet sign lettered with gold, and here a kaleidoscopic effect in the garments of a passer-by. Directly opposite, and two stories above their heads, a sort of huge "loggia," one blaze of gilding and crude vermilions, opened in the gray cement of a crumbling facade, like a sudden burst of flame. Gigantic pot-bellied lanterns of red and gold swung from its ceiling, while along its railing stood a row of pots—brass, ruddy bronze, and blue porcelain—from which were growing red saffron, purple, pink, and golden tulips without number. The air was vibrant with unfamiliar noises. From one of the balconies near at hand, though unseen, a gong, a pipe, and some kind of stringed instrument wailed and thundered in unison. There was a vast shuffling of padded soles and a continuous interchange of singsong monosyllables, high-pitched and staccato, while from every hand rose the strange aromas of the East—sandalwood, punk, incense, oil, and the smell of mysterious cookery.

"Chinatown!" exclaimed Travis. "I hadn't the faintest idea we had come up so far. Condy Rivers, do you know what time it is?" She pointed a white kid finger through the doorway of a drugstore, where, amid lacquer boxes and bronze urns of herbs and dried seeds, a round Seth Thomas marked half-past two.

"And your lunch?" cried Condy. "Great heavens! I never thought."

"It's too late to get any at home. Never mind; I'll go somewhere and have a cup of tea."

"Why not get a package of Chinese tea, now that you're down here, and take it home with you?"

"Or drink it here."

"Where?"

"In one of the restaurants. There wouldn't be a soul there at this hour. I know they serve tea any time. Condy, let's try it. Wouldn't it be fun?"

Condy smote his thigh. "Fun!" he vociferated. "Fun! It is—by Jove—it would be *heavenly!* Wait a moment. I'll tell you what we will do. Tea won't be enough. We'll go down to Kearney Street, or to the market, and get some crackers to go with it."

They hurried back to the California market, a few blocks distant, and bought some crackers and a wedge of new cheese. On the way back to Chinatown Travis stopped at a music store on Kearney Street to get her banjo, which she had left to have its head tightened; and thus burdened they regained the "town," Condy grieving audibly at having to carry "brown-paper bundles through the street."

"First catch your restaurant," said Travis as they turned into Dupont Street with its thronging coolies and swarming, gayly clad children. But they had not far to seek.

"Here you are!" suddenly exclaimed Condy, halting in front of a wholesale tea-house bearing a sign in Chinese and English. "Come on, Travis!"

They ascended two flights of a broad, brass-bound staircase leading up from the ground floor, and gained the restaurant on the top story of the building. As Travis had foretold, it was deserted. She clasped her gloved hands gayly, crying: "Isn't it delightful! We've the whole place to ourselves."

The restaurant ran the whole depth of the building, and was finished off at either extremity with a gilded balcony, one overlooking Dupont Street and the other the old Plaza. Enormous screens of gilded ebony, intricately carved and set with colored glass panes, divided the room into three, and one of these divisions, in the rear part, from which they could step out upon the balcony that commanded the view of the Plaza, they elected as their own.

It was charming. At their backs they had the huge, fantastic screen, brave and fine with its coat of gold. In front, through the glass-paned valves of a pair of folding doors, they could see the roofs of the houses beyond the Plaza, and beyond these the blue of the bay with its anchored ships, and even beyond this the faint purple of the Oakland shore. On either side of these doors, in deep alcoves, were divans with mattings and head-rests for opium smokers. The walls were painted blue and hung with vertical Cantonese legends in red and silver, while all around the sides of the room small ebony tables alternated with ebony stools, each inlaid with a slab of mottled marble. A chandelier, all a-glitter with tinsel, swung from the center of the ceiling over a huge round table of mahogany.

And not a soul was there to disturb them. Below them, out there around the old Plaza, the city drummed through its work with a lazy, soothing rumble. Nearer at hand, Chinatown sent up the vague murmur of the life of the Orient. In the direction of the Mexican quarter, the bell of the cathedral tolled at intervals. The sky was without a cloud and the afternoon was warm.

Condy was inarticulate with the joy of what he called their "discovery." He got up and sat down. He went out into the other room and came back again. He dragged up a couple of the marble-seated stools to the table. He took off his hat, lighted a cigarette, let it go out, lighted it again, and burned his fingers. He opened and closed the folding-doors, pushed the table into a better light, and finally brought Travis out upon the balcony to show her the "points of historical interest" in and around the

Plaza.

"There's the Stevenson memorial ship in the center, see; and right there, where the flagstaff is, General Baker made the funeral oration over the body of Terry. Broderick killed him in a duel—or was it Terry killed Broderick? I forget which. Anyhow, right opposite, where that pawnshop is, is where the Overland stages used to start in '49. And every other building that fronts on the Plaza, even this one we're in now, used to be a gambling-house in bonanza times; and, see, over yonder is the Morgue and the City Prison."

They turned back into the room, and a great, fat Chinaman brought them tea on Condy's order. But besides tea, he brought dried almonds, pickled watermelon rinds, candied quince, and "China nuts."

Travis cut the cheese into cubes with Condy's penknife, and arranged the cubes in geometric figures upon the crackers.

"But, Conde," she complained, "why in the world did you get so many crackers? There's hundreds of them here—enough to feed a regiment. Why didn't you ask me?"

"Huh! What? What? I don't know. What's the matter with the crackers? You were dickering with the cheese, and the man said, 'How many crackers?' I didn't know. I said, 'Oh, give me a quarter's worth!'"

"And we couldn't possibly have eaten ten cents' worth! Oh, Conde, you are—you are—But never mind, here's your tea. I wonder if this green, pasty stuff is good."

They found that it was, but so sweet that it made their tea taste bitter. The watermelon rinds were flat to their Western palates, but the dried almonds were a great success. Then Conde promptly got the hiccoughs from drinking his tea too fast, and fretted up and down the room like a chicken with the pip till Travis grew faint and weak with laughter.

"Oh, well," he exclaimed aggrievedly—"laugh, that's right! I don't laugh. It isn't such fun when you've got 'em yoursel'—*help!*"

"But sit down, for goodness' sake! You make me so nervous. You can't walk them off. Sit down and hold your breath while you count nine. Conde, I'm going to take off my gloves and veil. What do you think?"

"Sure, of course; and I'll have a cigarette. Do you mind if I smoke?"

"Well, what's that in your hand now?"

"By Jove, I have been smoking! I—I beg your pardon. I'm a regular stable boy. I'll throw it away."

Travis caught his wrist. "What nonsense! I would have told you before if I'd minded."

"But it's gone out!" he exclaimed. "I'll have another."

As he reached into his pocket for his case, his hand encountered a paper-covered volume. and he drew it out in some perplexity.

"Now, how in the wide world did that book come in my pocket?" he muttered, frowning. "What have I been carrying it around for? I've forgotten. I declare I have."

"What book is it?"

"Hey? book? . . . h'm," he murmured, staring.

Travis pounded on the table. "Wake up, Conde, I'm talking to you," she called.

"It's *Life's Handicap*," he answered, with a start; "but why and but why have I—"

"What's it about? I never heard of it," she declared.

"You never heard of *Life's Handicap*?" he shouted; "you never heard—you never—you mean to say you never heard—but here, this won't do. Sit right still, and I'll read you one of these yarns before you're another minute older. Any one of them—open the book at random. Here we are—'The Strange Ride of Morrowbie Jukes'; and it's a stem-winder, too."

And then for the first time in her life, there in that airy, golden Chinese restaurant, in the city from which she hastened to flee, Travis Bessemer fell under the charm of the little spectacled colonial, to whose song we all must listen and to whose pipe we all must dance.

There was one "point" in the story of Jukes' strange ride that Conde prided himself upon having discovered. So far as he knew, all critics had overlooked it. It is where Jukes is describing the man-trap of the City of the Dead who are alive, and mentions that the slope of the inclosing sand-hills was "about forty-five degrees." Jukes was a civil engineer, and Conde held that it was a capital bit of realism on the part of the author to have him speak of the pitch of the hills in just such technical terms. At first he thought he would call Travis' attention to this bit of cleverness; but as he read he abruptly changed his mind. He would see if she would find it out for herself. It would be a test of her quickness, he told himself; almost an unfair test, because the point was extremely subtle and could easily be ignored by the most experienced of fiction readers. He read steadily on, working himself into a positive excitement as he approached the passage. He came to it and read it through without any emphasis, almost slurring over it in his eagerness to be perfectly fair. But as he began to read the next paragraph, Travis, her little eyes sparkling with interest and attention, exclaimed:

"Just as an engineer would describe it. Isn't that good!"

"Glory hallelujah!" cried Conde, slamming down the book joyfully. "Travis, you are one in a thousand!"

"What—what is it?' she inquired blankly.

"Never mind, never mind; you're a wonder, that's all"—and he finished the tale without further explanation. Then, while he smoked another cigarette and she drank another cup of tea, he read to her "The Return of Imri" and the "Incarnation of Krishna Mulvaney." He found her an easy and enrapt convert to the little Englishman's creed, and for himself tasted the intense delight of revealing to another an appreciation of a literature hitherto ignored.

"Isn't he strong!" cried Travis. "Just a *little* better than Marie Corelli and the Duchess!"

"And to think of having all those stories to read! You haven't read any of them yet?"

"Not a one. I've been reading only the novels we take up in the Wednesday class."

"Lord!" muttered Conde.

Condy's spirits had been steadily rising since the incident aboard the whaleback. The exhilaration of the waterfront, his delight over the story he was to make out of the old mate's yarn, Chinatown, the charming unconventionality of their lunch in the Chinese restaurant, the sparkling serenity of the afternoon, and the joy of discovering Travis' appreciation of his adored and venerated author, had put him into a mood bordering close upon hilarity.

"The next event upon our interesting program," he announced, "will be a banjosephine obligato in A-sia minor, by that justly renowned impresario, Signor Conde Tin-pani Rivers, specially engaged for this performance; with a pleasing and panhellenic song-and-dance turn by Miss Travis Bessemer, the infant phenomenon, otherwise known as 'Babby Bessie.'"

"You're not going to play that banjo here?" said Travis, as he stripped away the canvas covering.

"Order in the gallery!" cried Conde, beginning to tune up. Then in a rapid, professional monotone: "Ladies—and—gentlemen—with—your—kind—permission—I -will—endeavor—to—give—you—an—imitation—of-a—Carolina—negro—song"—and without more ado, singing the words to a rattling, catchy accompaniment, swung off into—

"F-o-o-r *my* gal's a high-born leddy,

she's black, but not too shady."

He did not sing loud, and the clack and snarl of the banjo carried hardly further than the adjoining room; but there was no one to hear, and, as he went along, even Travis began to hum the words, but at that, Conde stopped abruptly, laid the instrument across his knees with exaggerated solicitude, and said deliberately:

"Travis, you are a good, sweet girl, and what you lack in beauty you make up in amiability, and I've no doubt you are kind to your aged father; but you can *not* sing."

Travis was cross in a moment, all the more so because Conde had spoken the exact truth. It was quite impossible for her to carry a tune half a dozen bars without entangling herself in as many different keys. What voice she had was not absolutely bad; but as she persisted in singing in spite of Condy's guying, he put back his head and began a mournful and lugubrious howling.

"Ho!" she exclaimed, grabbing the banjo from his knees, "if I can't sing, I can play better than some smart people."

"Yes, by note," rallied Conde, as Travis executed a banjo "piece" of no little intricacy. "That's just like a machine—like a hand-piano."

"Order in the gallery!" she retorted, without pausing in her playing. She finished with a great flourish and gazed at him in triumph, only to find him pretending a profound slumber. "O—o—o!" she remarked between her teeth, "I just hate you, Conde Rivers."

"There are others," he returned airily.

"Talk about slang."

"*Now* what will we do?" he cried. "Let's *do* something. Suppose we break something—just for fun."

Then suddenly the gaiety went out of his face, and he started up and clapped his hand to his head with a gasp of dismay. "Great Heavens!" he exclaimed.

"Conde," cried Travis in alarm, "what is it?"

"The Tea!" he vociferated. "Laurie Flagg's Tea. I ought to be there—right this minute."

Travis fetched a sigh of relief. "Is that all?"

"All!" he retorted. "All! Why, it's past four now—and I'd forgotten every last thing." Then suddenly falling calm again, and quietly resuming his seat: "I don't see as it makes any difference. I won't go, that's all. Push those almonds here, will you, Miss Lady?—But we aren't *doing* anything," he exclaimed, with a brusque return of exuberance. "Let's do things. What'll we do? Think of something. Is there anything we can break?" Then, without any transition, he vaulted upon the table and began to declaim, with tremendous gestures:

> "*There once was a beast called an Ounce,*
> *Who went with a spring and a bounce.*
> *His head was as flat*
> *As the head of a cat,*
> *This quadrupetantical Ounce.*
>
> *You'd think from his name he was small,*
> *But that was not like him at all.*
> *He weighed, I'll be bound,*
> *Three or four hundred pound,*
> *And he looked most uncommonly tall!*"

"Bravo! Bravo!" cried Travis, pounding on the table. "Hear, hear—bravo!"

Conde sat down on the table and swung his legs. But during the next few moments, while they were eating the last of their cheese, his good spirits fell rapidly away from him. He heaved a sigh and thrust both hands gloomily into his pockets.

"Cheese, Conde?" asked Travis.

He shook his head with a dark frown, muttering: "No cheese, no cheese."

"What's wrong, Condy—what's the matter?" asked Travis, with concern.

For some time he would not tell her, answering all her inquiries by closing his eyes and putting his chin in the air, nodding his head in knowing fashion.

"But what is it?"

"You don't respect me," he muttered; and for a long time this was all that could be got from him. No, no, she did not respect him; no, she did not take him seriously.

"But of course I do. Why don't I? Conde Rivers, what's got into you *now*?"

"No, no; I know it. I can tell. You don't take me seriously. You don't respect me."

"But why?"

"Make a blooming buffoon of myself," he mumbled tragically.

In great distress Travis labored to contradict him. Why, they had just been having a good time, that was all. Why, she had been just as silly as he. Conde caught at the word.

"Silly! There. I knew it. I told you. I'm silly. I'm a buffoon.—But haven't we had a great afternoon?" he added, with a sudden grin.

"I never remember," announced Travis emphatically, "when I've had a better time than I've had today; and I know just why it's been such a success."

"Why, then?"

"Because we've had no foolishness. We've just been ourselves, and haven't pretended we were in love with each other when we are not. Conde, let's do this lots."

"Do what?"

"Go round to queer little, interesting little places. We've had a glorious time today, haven't we?—and we haven't been talked out once."

"As we were last night, for instance," he hazarded.

"I *thought* you felt it, the same as I did. It *was* a bit awful wasn't it?"

"It was."

"From now on, let's make a resolution. I know you've had a good time today. Haven't you had a better time than if you had gone to the Tea?"

"Well, *rather*. I don't know when I've had a better, jollier afternoon."

"Well, now, we're going to try to have lots more good times, but just as chums. We've tried the other, and it failed. Now be sincere; didn't it fail?"

"It worked out. It *did* work out."

"Now from this time on, no more foolishness. We'll just be chums."

"Chums it is. No more foolishness."

"The moment you begin to pretend you're in love with me, it will spoil everything. It's funny," said Travis, drawing on her gloves. "We're doing a funny thing, Conde. With ninety-nine people out of one hundred, this little affair would have been all ended after our 'explanation' of last night—confessing, as we did, that we didn't love each other. Most couples would have 'drifted apart'; but here we are, planning to be chums, and have good times in our own original, unconventional way—and we can do it, too. There, there, he's a thousand miles away. He's not heard a single word I've said. Conde, are you listening to me?"

"Blix," he murmured, staring at her vaguely. "Blix—you look that way; I don't know, look kind of blix. Don't you feel sort of blix?" he inquired anxiously.

"Blix?"

He smote the table with his palm. "Capital!" he cried; "sounds bully, and snappy, and crisp, and bright, and sort of sudden. Sounds—don't you know, *this* way?"—and he snapped his fingers. "Don't you see what I mean? Blix, that's who you are. You've always been Blix, and I've just found it out. Blix," he added, listening to the sound of the name. "Blix, Blix. Yes, yes; that's your name."

"Blix?" she repeated; "but why Blix?"

"Why not?"

"I don't know why not."

"Well, then," he declared, as though that settled the question. They made ready to go, as it was growing late.

"Will you tie that for me, Conde," she asked, rising and turning the back of her head toward him, the ends of the veil held under her fingers. "Not too tight. Conde, don't pull it so tight. There, there, that will do. Have you everything that belongs to you? I know you'll go away and leave something here. There's your cigarette case, and your book, and of course the banjo."

As if warned by a mysterious instinct, the fat Chinaman made his appearance in the outer room. Conde put his fingers into his vest pocket, then dropped back upon his stool with a suppressed exclamation of horror.

"Conde!" exclaimed Blix in alarm, "are you sick?"—for he had turned a positive white.

"I haven't a cent of money," he murmured faintly. "I spent my last quarter for those beastly crackers. What's to be done? What is to be done? I'll—I'll leave him my watch. Yes, that's the only thing."

Blix calmly took out her purse. "I expected it," she said resignedly. "I knew this would happen sooner or later, and I always have been prepared. How much is it, John?" she asked of the Chinaman.

"Hefah dollah."

"I'll never be able to look you in the face again," protested Conde. "I'll pay you back tonight. I will! I'll send it up by a messenger boy."

"Then you *would* be a buffoon."

"Don't!" he exclaimed. "Don't, it humiliates me to the dust."

"Oh, come along and don't be so absurd. It must be after five."

Halfway down the brass-bound stairs, he clapped his hand to his head with a start.

"And *now* what is it?" she inquired meekly.

"Forgotten, forgotten!" he exclaimed. "I knew I would forget something."

"I knew it, you mean."

He ran back, and returned with the great bag of crackers, and thrust it into her hands. "Here, here, take these. We mustn't leave these," he declared earnestly. "It would be a shameful waste of money;" and in spite of all her protests, he insisted upon taking the crackers along.

"I wonder," said Blix, as the two skirted the Plaza, going down to Kearney Street; "I wonder if I ought to ask him to supper?"

"Ask who—me?—how funny to—"

"I wonder if we are talked out—if it would spoil the day?"

"Anyhow, I'm going to have supper at the Club; and I've got to write my article some time tonight."

Blix fixed him with a swift glance of genuine concern. "Don't play tonight, Conde," she said, with a sudden gravity.

"Fat lot I can play! What money have I got to play with?"

"You might get some somewheres. But, anyhow, promise me you won't play."

"Well, of course I'll promise. How can I, if I haven't any money? And besides, I've got my whaleback stuff to write. I'll have supper at the Club, and go up in the library and grind out copy for a while."

"Conde," said Blix, "I think that diver's story is almost too good for *The Times*. Why don't you write it and send it East? Send it to the Centennial Company, why don't you? They've paid some attention to you now, and it would keep your name in their minds if you sent the story to them, even if they didn't publish it. Why don't you think of that?"

"Fine—great idea! I'll do that. Only I'll have to write it out of business hours. It will be extra work."

"Never mind, you do it; and," she added, as he put her on the cable car, "keep your mind on that thirty-thousand-word story of adventure. Good-bye, Conde; haven't we had the jolliest day that ever was?"

"Couldn't have been better. Good-bye, Blix."

Conde returned to his club. It was about six o'clock. In response to his question, the hall-boy told him that Tracy Sargeant had arrived a few moments previous, and had been asking for him.

The Saturday of the week before, Conde had made an engagement with young Sargeant to have supper together that night, and perhaps go to the theater afterward. And now at the sight of Sargeant in the "round window" of the main room, buried in the file of the "Gil Blas," Conde was pleased to note that neither of them had forgotten the matter.

Sargeant greeted him with extreme cordiality as he came up, and at once proposed a drink. Sargeant was a sleek, well-groomed, well-looking fellow of thirty, just beginning to show the effects of a certain amount of dissipation in the little puffs under the eyes and the faint blueness of the temples. The sudden death of his father for which event Sargeant was still mourning, had left him in such position that his monthly income was about five times as large as Condy's salary. The two had supper together, and Sargeant proposed the theater.

"No, no; I've got to work tonight," asserted Conde.

After dinner, while they were smoking their cigars in a window of the main room, one of the hall-boys came up and touched Conde on the arm.

"Mr. Eckert, and Mr. Hendricks, and Mr. George Hands, and several other of those gentlemen are up in the card-room, and are asking for you and Mr. Sargeant."

"Why, I didn't know the boys were here! They've got a game going, Conde. Let's go up and get in. Shall we?"

Conde remembered that he had no money. "I'm flat broke, Tracy," he announced, for he knew Sargeant well enough to make the confession without wincing. "No, I'll not get in; but I'll go up and watch you a few minutes."

They ascended to the card-room, where the air was heavy and acrid with cigar smoke, and where the silence was broken only by the click of poker-chips. At the end of twenty minutes Conde was playing, having borrowed enough money of Sargeant to start him in the game.

Unusually talkative and restless, he had suddenly hardened and stiffened to a repressed, tense calm; speechless, almost rigid in his chair. Excitable under even ordinary circumstances, his every faculty was now keyed to its highest pitch. The nervous strain upon him was like the stretching and tightening of harp-strings, too taut to quiver. The color left his face, and the moisture fled his lips. His projected article, his promise to Blix, all the jollity of the afternoon, all thought of time or place, faded away as the one indomitable, evil passion of the man leaped into life within him, and lashed and roweled him with excitement. His world resolved itself to a round green table, columns of tri-colored chips, and five ever-changing cards that came and went and came again before his tired eyes like the changing, weaving colors of the kaleidoscope. Midnight struck, then one o'clock, then two, three, and four. Still his passion rode him like a hag, spurring the jaded body, rousing up the wearied brain.

Finally, at half-past four, at a time when Conde was precisely where he had started, neither winner nor loser by so much as a dime, a round of Jackpots was declared, and the game broke up. Conde walked home to the uptown hotel where he lived with his mother, and went to bed as the first milk-wagons began to make their appearance and the newsboys to cry the morning papers.

Then, as his tired eyes closed at last, occurred that strange trick of picture-making that the overtaxed brain plays upon the retina. A swift series of pictures of the day's doings began to whirl *through* rather than *before* the pupils of his shut eyes. Conde saw again a brief vision of the street, and Blix upon the corner waiting to cross; then it was the gay, brisk confusion of the waterfront, the old mate's cabin aboard the whaleback, Chinatown, and a loop of vermilion cloth over a gallery rail, the golden balcony, the glint of the Stevenson ship upon the green Plaza, Blix playing the banjo, the delightful and picturesque confusion of the deserted Chinese restaurant; Blix again, turning her head for him to fasten her veil, holding the ends with her white-kid fingers; Blix once more, walking at his side with her trim black skirt, her round little turban hat, her yellow hair, and her small dark, dancing eyes.

Then, suddenly, he remembered the promise he had made her in the matter of playing that night. He winced sharply at this, and the remembrance of his fault harried and harassed him. In spite of himself, he felt contemptible. Yet he had broken his promises to her in this very matter of playing before—before that day of their visit to the Chinese restaurant—and had felt no great qualm of self-reproach. Had their relations changed? Rather the reverse for they had done with "foolishness."

"Never worried me before," muttered Conde, as he punched up his pillow. "Never worried me before. Why should it worry me now—worry me like the devil; and she caught on to that 'point' about the slope of forty-five degrees."

Chapter V

Conde began his week's work for the supplement behindhand. Naturally he overslept himself Tuesday morning, and, not having any change in his pockets, was obliged to walk down to the office. He arrived late, to find the compositors already fretting for copy. His editor promptly asked for the whaleback stuff, and Conde was forced into promising it within a half-hour. It was out of the question to write the article according to his own idea in so short a time; so Conde faked the stuff from the exchange clipping, after all. His description of the boat and his comments upon her mission—taken largely at second hand—served only to fill space in the paper. They were lacking both in interest and in point. There were no illustrations. The article was a failure.

But Conde redeemed himself by a witty interview later in the week with an emotional actress, and by a solemn article compiled after an hour's reading in Lafcadio Hearn and the Encyclopedia—on the "Industrial Renaissance in Japan."

But the idea of the diver's story came back to him again and again, and Thursday night after supper he went down to his club, and hid himself at a corner desk in the library, and, in a burst of enthusiasm, wrote out some two thousand words of it. In order to get the "technical details," upon which he set such store, he consulted the Encyclopedias again, and "worked in" a number of unfamiliar phrases and odd-sounding names. He was so proud of the result that he felt he could not wait until the tale was finished and in print to try its effect. He wanted appreciation and encouragement upon the instant. He thought of Blix.

"She saw the point in Morrowbie Jukes' description of the slope of the sand-hill," he told himself; and the next moment had resolved to go up and see her the next evening, and read to her what he had written.

This was on Thursday. All through that week Blix had kept much to herself, and for the first time in two years had begun to spend every evening at home. In the morning of each day she helped Victorine with the upstairs work, making the beds, putting the rooms to rights; or consulted with the butcher's and grocer's boys at the head of the back stairs, or chaffered with urbane and smiling Chinamen with their balanced vegetable baskets. She knew the house and its management at her fingers' ends, and supervised everything that went forward. Laurie Flagg coming to call upon her, on Wednesday afternoon, to remonstrate upon her sudden defection, found her in the act of tacking up a curtain across the pantry window.

But Blix had the afternoons and evenings almost entirely to herself. These hours, heretofore taken up with functions and the discharge of obligations, dragged not a little during the week that followed upon her declaration of independence. Wednesday afternoon, however, was warm and fine, and she went to the Park with Snooky. Without looking for it or even expecting it, Blix came across a little Japanese tea-house, or rather a tiny Japanese garden, set with almost toy Japanese houses and pavilions, where tea was served and thin sweetish wafers for five cents. Blix and Snooky went in. There was nobody about but the Japanese serving woman. Snooky was in raptures, and Blix spent a delightful half-hour there, drinking Japanese tea, and feeding the wafers to the carp and gold-fish in the tiny pond immediately below where she sat. A Chinaman, evidently of the merchant class, came in, with a Chinese woman following. As he took his place and the Japanese girl came up to get his order, Blix overheard him say in English: "Bring tea for-um leddy."

"He had to speak in English to her," she whispered; "isn't that splendid! Did you notice that, Snooky?"

On the way home Blix was wondering how she should pass her evening. She was to have made one of a theater party where Jack Carter was to be present. Then she suddenly remembered "Morrowbie Jukes," "The Return of Imri," and "Krishna Mulvaney." She continued on past her home, downtown, and returned late for supper with "Plain Tales" and "Many Inventions."

Toward half-past eight there came a titter of the electric bell. At the moment Blix was in the upper chamber of the house of Suddhoo, quaking with exquisite horror at the Seal-cutter's magic. She looked up quickly as the bell rang. It was not Conde Rivers' touch. She swiftly reflected that it was Wednesday night, and that she might probably expect Frank Catlin. He was a fair specimen of the Younger Set, a sort of modified Jack Carter, and called upon her about once a fortnight. No doubt he would hint darkly as to his riotous living during the past few days and refer to his diet of bromo-seltzers. He would be slangy, familiar, call her by her first name as many times as he dared, discuss the last dance of the Saturday cotillion, and try to make her laugh over Carter's drunkenness. Blix knew the type. Catlin was hardly out of college; but the older girls, even the young women of twenty-five or six, encouraged and petted these youngsters, driven to the alternative by the absolute dearth of older men.

"I'm not at home, Victorine," announced Blix, intercepting the maid in the hall. It chanced that it was not Frank Catlin, but another boy of precisely the same breed; and Blix returned to Suddhoo, Mrs. Hawksbee, and Mulvaney with a little cuddling movement of satisfaction.

"There is only one thing I regret about this," she said to Conde Rivers on the Friday night of that week; "that is, that I never thought of doing it before." Then suddenly she put up her hand to shield her eyes, as though from an intense light, turning away her head abruptly.

"I say, what is it? What—what's the matter?" he exclaimed.

Blix peeped at him fearfully from between her fingers. "He's got it on," she whispered, "that awful crimson scarf."

"Hoh!" said Conde, touching his scarf nervously, "it's—it's very swell. Is it too loud?" he asked uneasily.

Blix put her fingers in her ears; then:

"Conde, you're a nice, amiable young man, and, if you're not brilliant, you're good and kind to your aged mother; but your scarfs and neckties are simply impossible."

"Well, look at this room!" he shouted—they were in the parlor. "You needn't talk about bad taste. Those drapes—oh-h! those drapes!! Yellow, s'help me! And those bisque figures that you get with every pound of tea you buy; and this, this, *this*," he whimpered, waving his hands at the decorated sewer-pipe with its gilded cattails. "Oh, speak to me of this; speak to me of art; speak to me of aesthetics. Cattails, *gilded*. Of course, why not *gilded*!" He wrung his hands. "'Somewhere people are happy. Somewhere little children are at play—'"

"Oh, hush!" she interrupted. "I know it's bad; but we've always had it so, and I won't have it abused. Let's go into the dining-room, anyway. We'll sit in there after this. We've always been stiff and constrained in here."

They went out into the dining-room, drew up a couple of arm-chairs into the bay window, and sat there looking out. Blix had not yet lighted the gas—it was hardly dark enough for that; and for upward of ten minutes they sat and watched the evening dropping into night.

Below them the hill fell away so abruptly that the roofs of the nearest houses were almost at their feet; and beyond these the city tumbled raggedly down to meet the bay in a confused, vague mass of roofs, cornices, cupolas, and chimneys, blurred and indistinct in the twilight, but here and there pierced by a new-lighted street lamp. Then came the bay. To the east they could see Goat Island, and the fleet of sailing-ships anchored off the waterfront; while directly in their line of vision the island of Alcatraz, with its triple crown of forts, started from the surface of the water. Beyond was the Contra Costa shore, a vast streak of purple against the sky. The eye followed its sky-line westward till it climbed, climbed, climbed up a long slope that suddenly leaped heavenward with the crest of Tamalpais, purple and still, looking always to the sunset like a great watching sphinx. Then, further on, the slope seemed to break like the breaking of an advancing billow, and go tumbling, crumbling downward to meet the Golden Gate—the narrow inlet of green tide-water with its flanking Presidio. But, further than this, the eye was stayed. Further than this there was nothing, nothing but a vast, illimitable plain of green—the open Pacific. But at this hour the color of the scene was its greatest charm. It glowed with all the somber radiance of a cathedral. Everything was seen through a haze of purple—from the low green hills in the Presidio Reservation to the faint red mass of Mount Diablo shrugging its rugged shoulder over the Contra Costa foot-hills. As the evening faded, the west burned down to a dull red glow that overlaid the blue of the bay with a sheen of ruddy gold. The foot-hills of the opposite shore, Diablo, and at last even Tamalpais, resolved themselves in the velvet gray of the sky. Outlines were lost. Only the masses remained, and these soon began to blend into one another. The sky, and land, and the city's huddled roofs were one. Only the sheen of dull gold remained, piercing the single vast mass of purple like the blade of a golden sword.

"There's a ship!" said Blix in a low tone.

A four-master was dropping quietly through the Golden Gate, swimming on that sheen of gold, a mere shadow, specked with lights red and green. In a few moments her bows were shut from sight by the old fort at the Gate. Then her red light vanished, then the mainmast. She was gone. By midnight she would be out of sight of land, rolling on the swell of the lonely ocean under the moon's white eye.

Conde and Blix sat quiet and without speech, not caring to break the charm of the evening. For quite five minutes they sat thus, watching the stars light one by one, and the immense gray night settle and broaden and widen from mountaintop to horizon. They did not feel the necessity of making conversation. There was no constraint in their silence now.

Gently, and a little at a time, Conde turned his head and looked at Blix. There was just light enough to see. She was leaning back in her chair, her hands fallen into her lap, her head back and a little to one side. As usual, she was in black; but now it was some sort of dinner-gown that left her arms and neck bare. The line of the chin and the throat and the sweet round curve of the shoulder had in it something indescribable—something that was related to music, and that eluded speech. Her hair was nothing more than a warm colored mist without form or outline. The sloe-brown of her little eyes and the flush of her cheek were mere inferences—like the faintest stars that are never visible when looked at directly; and it seemed to him that there was disengaged from her something for which there was no name; something that appealed to a mysterious sixth sense—a sense that only stirred at such quiet moments as this; something that was now a dim, sweet radiance, now a faint aroma, and now again a mere essence, an influence, an impression—nothing more. It seemed to him as if her sweet, clean purity and womanliness took a form of its own which his accustomed senses were too gross to perceive. Only a certain vague tenderness in him went out to meet and receive this impalpable presence; a tenderness not for her only, but for all the good things of the world. Often he had experienced the same feeling when listening to music. Her sweetness, her goodness, appealed to what he guessed must be the noblest in him. And she was only nineteen. Suddenly his heart swelled, the ache came to his throat and the smart to his eyes.

"Blixy," he said, just above a whisper; "Blixy, wish I was a better sort of chap."

"That's the beginning of being better, isn't it, Conde?" she answered, turning toward him, her chin on her hand.

"It does seem a pity," he went on, "that when you *want* to do the right, straight thing, and be clean and fine, that you can't just *be* it, and have it over with. It's the keeping it up that's the grind."

"But it's the keeping it up, Conde, that makes you *worth being good* when you finally get to be good; don't you think? It's the keeping it up that makes you strong; and then when you get to be good you can make your goodness count. What's a good man if he's weak?—if his goodness is better than he is himself? It's the good man who is strong—as strong as his goodness, and who can make his goodness count—who is the right kind of man. That's what I think."

"There's something in that, there's something in that." Then, after a pause: "I played Monday night, after all, Blix, after promising I wouldn't."

For a time she did not answer, and when she spoke, she spoke quietly: "Well—I'm glad you told me"; and after a little she added, "Can't you stop, Conde?"

"Why, yes—yes, of course—I—oh, Blix, sometimes I don't know! You can't understand! How could a girl understand the power of it? Other things, I don't say; but when it comes to gambling, there seems to be another me that does precisely as he chooses, whether I will or not. But I'm going to do my best. I haven't played since, although there was plenty of chance. You see, this card business is only a part of this club life, this city life—like drinking and—other vices of men. If I didn't have to lead the life, or if I didn't go with that crowd—Sargeant and the rest of those men—it would be different; easier, maybe."

"But a man ought to be strong enough to be himself and master of himself anywhere. Conde, *is* there anything in the world better or finer than a strong man?"

"Not unless it is a good woman, Blix."

"I suppose I look at it from a woman's point of view; but for me a *strong* man—strong in everything—is the grandest thing in the world. Women love strong men, Conde. They can forgive a strong man almost anything."

Conde did not immediately answer, and in the interval an idea occurred to Blix that at once hardened into a determination. But she said nothing at the moment. The spell of the sunset was gone and they had evidently reached the end of that subject of their talk. Blix rose to light the gas.

"Will you promise me one thing, Conde?" she said. "Don't if you don't want to. But will you promise me that you will tell me whenever you do play?"

"That I'll promise you!" exclaimed Conde; "and I'll keep that, too."

"And now, let's hear the story—or what you've done of it."

They drew up to the dining-room table with its cover of blue denim edged with white cord, and Conde unrolled his manuscript and read through what he had written. She approved, and, as he had foreseen, "caught on" to every one of his points. He was almost ready to burst into cheers when she said:

"Any one reading that would almost believe you had been a diver yourself, or at least had lived with divers. Those little details count, don't they? Conde, I've an idea. See what you think of it. Instead of having the story end with his leaving her down there and going away, do it this way. Let him leave her there, and then go back after a long time when he gets to be an old man. Fix it up some way to make it natural. Have him go down to see her and never come up again, see? And leave the reader in doubt as to whether it was an accident or whether he did it on purpose."

Conde choked back a whoop and smote his knee. "Blix, you're the eighth wonder! Magnificent—glorious! Say!"—he fixed her with a glance of curiosity—"you ought to take to story-writing yourself."

"No, no," she retorted significantly. "I'll just stay with my singing and be content with that. But remember that story don't go to *The Times* supplement. At least not until you have tried it East—with the Centennial Company, at any rate."

"Well, I guess *not!*" snorted Conde. "Why, this is going to be one of the best yarns I ever wrote."

A little later on he inquired with sudden concern: "Have you got anything to eat in the house?"

"I never saw such a man!" declared Blix; "you are always hungry."

"I love to eat," he protested.

"Well, we'll make some creamed oysters; how would that do?" suggested Blix.

Conde rolled his eyes. "Oh, speak to me of creamed oysters!" Then, with abrupt solemnity: "Blix, I never in my life had as many oysters as I could eat."

She made the creamed oysters in the kitchen over the gas-stove, and they ate them there—Conde sitting on the washboard of the sink, his plate in his lap.

Conde had a way of catching up in his hands whatever happened to be nearest him, and, while still continuing to talk, examining it with apparent deep interest. Just now it happened to be the morning's paper that Victorine had left on the table. For five minutes Conde had been picking it up and laying it down, frowning abstractedly at it during the pauses in the conversation. Suddenly he became aware of what it was, and instantly read aloud the first item that caught his glance:

"'Personal.—Young woman, thirty-one, good housekeeper, desires acquaintance respectable middle-aged gentleman. Object, matrimony. Address K. D. B., this office.'—Hum!" he commented, "nothing equivocal about K. D. B.; has the heroism to call herself young at thirty-one. I'll bet she *is* a good housekeeper. Right to the point. If K. D. B. don't see what she wants, she asks for it."

"I wonder," mused Blix, "what kind of people they are who put personals in the papers. K. D. B., for instance; who is she, and what is she like?"

"They're not tough," Conde assured her. "I see 'em often down at *The Times'* office. They are usually a plain, matter-of-fact sort, quite conscientious, you know; generally middle-aged—or thirty-one; outgrown their youthful follies and illusions, and want to settle down."

"Read some more," urged Blix. Conde went on.

"'Bachelor, good habits, twenty-five, affectionate disposition, accomplishments, money, desires acquaintance pretty, refined girl. Object, matrimony. McB., this office.'"

"No, I don't like McB.," said Blix. "He's too—ornamental, somehow."

"He wouldn't do for K. D. B., would he?"

"Oh, my, no! He'd make her very unhappy."

"'Widower, two children, home-loving disposition, desires introduction to good, honest woman to make home for his children. Matrimony, if suitable. B. P. T., Box A, this office.'"

"He's not for K. D. B., that's flat," declared Blix; "the idea, 'matrimony if suitable'—patronizing enough! I know just what kind of an old man B. P. T. is. I know he would want K. D. B. to warm his slippers, and would be fretful and grumpy. B. P. T., just an abbreviation of bumptious. No, he can't have her."

Conde read the next two or three to himself, despite her protests.

"Conde, don't be mean! Read them to—"

"Ah!" he exclaimed, "here's one for K. D. B. Behold, the bridegroom cometh! Listen."

"'Bachelor, thirty-nine, sober and industrious, retired sea captain, desires acquaintance respectable young woman, good housekeeper and manager. Object, matrimony. Address Captain Jack, office this paper.'"

"I know he's got a wooden leg!" cried Blix. "Can't you just see it sticking out between the lines? And he lives all alone somewhere down near the bay with a parrot—"

"And makes a glass of grog every night."

"And smokes a long clay pipe."

"But he chews tobacco."

"Yes, isn't it a pity he will chew that nasty, smelly tobacco? But K. D. B. will break him of that."

"Oh, is he for K. D. B.?"

"Sent by Providence!" declared Blix. "They were born for each other. Just see, K. D. B. is a good housekeeper, and wants a respectable middle-aged gentleman. Captain Jack is a respectable middle-aged gentleman, and wants a good housekeeper. Oh, and besides, I can read between the lines! I just feel they would be congenial. If they know what's best for themselves, they would write to each other right away."

"But wouldn't you love to be there and see them meet!" exclaimed Conde.

"Can't we fix it up some way," said Blix, "to bring these two together—to help them out in some way?"

Conde smote the table and jumped to his feet.

"Write to 'em!" he shouted. "Write to K. D. B. and sign it Captain Jack, and write to Captain Jack—"

"And sign it K. D. B.," she interrupted, catching his idea.

"And have him tell her, and her tell him," he added, "to meet at some place; and then we can go to that place and hide, and watch."

"But how will we know them? How would they know each other? They've never met."

"We'll tell them both to wear a kind of flower. Then we can know them, and they can know each other. Of course as soon as they began to talk they would find out they hadn't written."

"But they wouldn't care."

"No—they want to meet each other. They would be thankful to us for bringing them together."

"Won't it be the greatest fun?"

"Fun! Why, it will be a regular drama. Only we are running the show, and everything is real. Let's get at it!"

Blix ran into her room and returned with writing material. Conde looked at the note-paper critically. "This kind's too swell. K. D. B. wouldn't use Irish linen—never! Here, this is better, glazed with blue lines and a flying bird stamped in the corner. Now I'll write for the Captain, and you write for K. D. B."

"But where will we have them meet?"

This was a point. They considered the Chinese restaurant, the Plaza, Lotta's fountain, the Mechanics' Library, and even the cathedral over in the Mexican quarter, but arrived at no decision.

"Did you ever hear of Luna's restaurant?" said Conde. "By Jove, it's just the place! It's the restaurant where you get Mexican dinners; right in the heart of the Latin quarter; quiet little old-fashioned place, below the level of the street, respectable as a tomb. I was there just once. We'll have 'em meet there at seven in the evening. No one is there at that hour. The place isn't patronized much, and it shuts up at eight. You and I can go there and have dinner at six, say, and watch for them to come."

Then they set to work at their letters.

"Now," said Conde, "we must have these sound perfectly natural, because if either of these people smell the smallest kind of a rat, you won't catch 'em. You must write not as *You* would write, but as you think *they* would. This is an art, a kind of fiction, don't you see? We must imagine a certain character, and write a letter consistent with that character. Then it'll sound natural. Now, K. D. B. Well, K. D. B., she's prim. Let's have her prim, and proud of using correct, precise, 'elegant' language. I guess she wears mitts, and believes in cremation. Let's have her believe in cremation. And Captain Jack; oh!—he's got a terrible voice, like this, *row-row-row* see? and whiskers, very fierce; and he says, 'Belay there!' and 'Avast!' and is very grandiloquent and orotund and gallant when it comes to women. Oh, he's the devil of a man when it comes to women, is Captain Jack!"

After countless trials and failures, they evolved the two following missives, which Conde posted that night:

Captain Jack.

SIR:

I have perused with entire satisfaction your personal in *The Times*. I should like to know more of you. I read between the lines, and my perception ineradicably convinces me that you are honest and respectable. I do not believe I should compromise my self-esteem at all in granting you an interview. I shall be at Luna's restaurant at seven precisely, next Monday eve, and will bear a bunch of white marguerites. Will you likewise, and wear a marguerite in your lapel?
Trusting this will find you in health, I am
Respectfully yours,
K. D. B.

Miss K. D. B.

DEAR MISS:

From the modest and retiring description of your qualities and character, I am led to believe that I will find in you an agreeable life companion. Will you not accord me the great favor of a personal interview? I shall esteem it a high honor. I will be at Luna's Mexican restaurant at seven of the clock P.M. on Monday evening next. May I express the fervent hope that you also will be there? I name the locality because it is quiet and respectable. I shall wear a white marguerite in my buttonhole. Will you also carry a bunch of the same flower?
Yours to command,
Captain Jack.

So great was her interest in the affair that Blix even went out with Conde while he mailed the letters in the nearest box, for he was quite capable of forgetting the whole matter as soon as he was out of the house.

"Now let it work!" she exclaimed as the iron flap clanked down upon the disappearing envelopes. But Conde was suddenly smitten with name-less misgiving. "Now we've done it! Now we've done it!" he cried aghast. "I wish we hadn't. We're in a fine fix now."

Still uneasy, he saw Blix back to the flat, and bade her good-bye at the door.

But before she went to bed that night, Blix sought out her father, who was still sitting up tinkering with the cuckoo clock, which he had taken all to pieces under the pretext that it was out of order and went too fast.

"Papum," said Blix, sitting down on the rug before him, "did you ever—when you were a pioneer, when you first came out here in the fifties—did you ever play poker?"

"I—oh, well! It was the only amusement the miners had for a long time."

"I want you to teach me."

The old man let the clock fall into his lap and stared. But Blix explained her reasons.

Chapter VI

The next day was Saturday, and Blix had planned a walk out to the Presidio. But at breakfast, while she was debating whether she should take with her Howard and Snooky, or "Many Inventions," she received a note from Conde, sent by special messenger:

"'All our fun is spoiled,' he wrote. 'I've got ptomaine poisoning from eating the creamed oysters last night, and am in for a solid fortnight spent in bed. Have passed a horrible night. Can't you look in at the hotel this afternoon? My mother will be here at the time.'"

"Ptomaine poisoning!" The name had an ugly sound, and Condy's use of the term inferred the doctor's visit. Blix decided that she would put off her walk until the afternoon, and call on Mrs. Rivers at once, and ask how Conde did.

She got away from the flat about ten o'clock, but on the steps outside met Conde dressed as if for bicycling, and smoking a cigarette.

"I've got eleven dollars!" he announced cheerily.

"But I thought it was ptomaine poisoning!" she cried with sudden vexation.

"Pshaw! That's what the doctor says. He's a flapdoodle; nothing but a kind of a sort of a pain. It's all gone now. I'm as fit as a fiddle—and I've got eleven dollars. Let's go somewhere and do something."

"But your work?"

"They don't expect me. When I thought I was going to be sick, I telephoned the office, and they said all right, that they didn't need me. Now I've got eleven dollars, and there are three holidays of perfect weather before us: today, tomorrow, and Monday. What will we do? What must we do to be saved? Our matrimonial objects don't materialize till Monday night. In the meanwhile, what? Shall we go down to Chinatown—to the restaurant, or to the waterfront again? Maybe the mate on the whaleback would invite us to lunch. Or," added Conde, his eye caught by a fresh-fish peddler who had just turned into the street, "we can go fishing."

"For oysters, perhaps."

But the idea had caught Condy's fancy.

"Blix!" he exclaimed, "let's go fishing."

"Where?"

"I don't know. Where *do* people fish around here? Where there's water, I presume."

"No, is it possible?" she asked with deep concern. "I thought they

51

fished in their back yards, or in their front parlors perhaps."

"Oh, you be quiet! you're all the time guying me," he answered. "Let me think—let me think," he went on, frowning heavily, scouring at his hair. Suddenly he slapped a thigh.

"Come on," he cried, "I've an idea!" He was already halfway down the steps, when Blix called him back.

"Leave it all to me," he assured her; "trust me *implicitly*. Don't you want to go?" he demanded with abrupt disappointment.

"Want to!" she exclaimed. "Why, it would be the very best kind of fun, but—"

"Well, then, come along."

They took a downtown car.

"I've got a couple of split bamboo rods," he explained as the car slid down the terrific grade of the Washington-Street hill. "I haven't used 'em in years—not since we lived East; but they're handmade, and are tip-top. I haven't any other kind of tackle; but it's just as well, because the tackle will all depend upon where we are going to fish."

"Where's that?"

"Don't know yet; am going down now to find out."

He took her down to the principal dealer in sporting goods on Market Street. It was a delicious world, whose atmosphere and charm were not to be resisted. There were shotguns in rows, their gray barrels looking like so many organ-pipes; sheaves of fishing-rods, from the four-ounce wisp of the brook-trout up to the rigid eighteen-ounce lance of the king-salmon and sea-bass; showcases of wicked revolvers, swelling by calibers into the thirty-eight and forty-four man-killers of the plainsmen and Arizona cavalry; hunting knives and dirks, and the slender steel whips of the fencers; files of Winchesters, sleeping quietly in their racks, waiting patiently for the signal to speak the one grim word they knew; swarms of artificial flies of every conceivable shade, brown, gray, black, gray-brown, gray-black, with here and there a brisk vermilion note; coils of line, from the thickness of a pencil, spun to hold the sullen plunges of a jew-fish off the Catalina Islands, down to the sea-green gossamers that a vigorous fingerling might snap; hooks, snells, guts, leaders, gaffs, cartridges, shells, and all the entrancing munitions of the sportsman, that savored of lonely canons, deer-licks, mountain streams, quail uplands, and the still reaches of inlet and marsh grounds, gray and cool in the early autumn dawn.

Conde and Blix got the attention of a clerk, and Conde explained.

"I want to go fishing—we want to go fishing. We want some place where we can go and come in the same day, and we want to catch fair-sized fish—no minnows."

The following half hour was charming. Never was there a clerk more delightful. It would appear that his one object in life was that Conde and Blix should catch fish. The affairs of the nation stood still while he pondered, suggested, advised, and deliberated. He told them where to go, how to get there, what train to take coming back, and who to ask for when they arrived. They would have to wait till Monday before going, but could return long before the fated hour of 7 P.M.

"Ask for Richardson," said the clerk; "and here, give him my card. He'll put you on to the good spots; some places are A-1 today, and tomorrow in the same place you can't kill a single fish."

Conde nudged Blix as the Mentor turned away to get his card.

"Notice that," he whispered. "*Kill* a fish. You don't say 'catch,' you say 'kill'—technical detail."

Then they bought their tackle: a couple of cheap reels, lines, leaders, sinkers, a book of assorted flies that the delightful clerk suggested, and a beautiful little tin box painted green, and stenciled with a gorgeous gold trout upon the lid, in which they were to keep the pint of salted shrimps to be used as bait in addition to the flies. Blix would get these shrimps at a little market near her home.

"But," said the clerk, "you got to get a permit to fish in that lake. Have you got a pull with the Water Company? Are you a stockholder?"

Condy's face fell, and Blix gave a little gasp of dismay. They looked at each other. Here was a check, indeed.

"Well," said the sublime being in shirt sleeves from behind the counter, "see what you can do; and if you can't make it, come back here an' lemme know, and we'll fix you up in some other place. But Lake San Andreas has been bang-up this last week—been some great kills there; hope to the deuce you can make it."

Everything now hinged upon this permit. It was not until their expedition had been in doubt that Conde and Blix realized how alluring had been its prospects.

"Oh, I guess you can get a permit," said the clerk soothingly. "An' if you make any good kills, lemme know and I'll put it in the paper. I'm the editor of the 'Sport-with-Gun-and-Rod' column in *The Press*," he added with a flush of pride.

Toward the middle of the afternoon Blix, who was waiting at home, in great suspense, for that very purpose, received another telegram from Conde:

> Tension of situation relieved. Unconditional permission obtained. Don't forget the shrimps.

It had been understood that Conde was to come to the flat on Sunday afternoon to talk over final arrangements with Blix. But as it was, Saturday evening saw him again at the Bessemers.

He had been down at his club in the library, writing the last paragraphs of his diver's story, when, just as he finished, Sargeant discovered him.

"Why, Conny, old man, all alone here? Let's go downstairs and have a cigar. Hendricks and George Hands are coming around in half an hour. They told me not to let you get away."

Conde stirred nervously in his chair. He knew what that meant. He had enough money in his pockets to play that night, and in an instant the enemy was all awake. The rowel was in his flank again, and the scourge at his back. Sargeant stood there, the well-groomed clubman of thirty; a little cynical perhaps, but a really good fellow for all that, and undeniably fond of Conde. But somewhere with the eyes of some second self Conde saw the girl of nineteen, part child and part woman; saw her goodness, her fine, sweet feminine strength as it were a dim radiance; "What's a good man worth, Conde," she had said, "if he's not a strong man?"

"I suppose we'll have a game going before midnight," admitted Sargeant resignedly, smiling good-humoredly nevertheless.

Conde set his teeth. "I'll join you later. Wait a few moments," he said. He hurried to the office of the club, and sent a despatch to Blix—the third since morning:

> Can I come up right away? It's urgent. Send answer by this messenger.

He got his answer within three-quarters of an hour, and left the club as Hendricks and George Hands arrived by the elevator entrance.

Sitting in the bay window of the dining-room, he told Blix why he had come.

"Oh, you were right!" she told him. "Always, *always* come, when—when you feel you must."

"It gets so bad sometimes, Blix," he confessed with abject self-contempt, "that when I can't get some one to play against I'll sit down and deal dummy hands, and bet on them. Just the touch of the cards—just the *feel* of the chips. Faugh! it's shameful."

The day following, Sunday, Conde came to tea as usual; and after the meal, as soon as the family and Victorine had left the pair alone in the dining-room, they set about preparing for their morrow's excursion. Blix put up their lunch—sandwiches of what Conde called "devilish" ham, hard-boiled eggs, stuffed olives, and a bottle of claret.

Conde took off his coat and made a great show of stringing the tackle: winding the lines from the spools on to the reels, and attaching the sinkers and flies to the leaders, smoking the while, and scowling fiercely. He got the lines fearfully and wonderfully snarled, he caught the hooks in the tablecloth, he lost the almost invisible gut leaders on the floor and looped the sinkers on the lines when they should have gone on the leaders. In the end Blix had to help him out, disentangling the lines foot by foot with a patience that seemed to Conde little short of superhuman.

At nine o'clock she said decisively:

"Do you know what time we must get up in the morning if we are to have breakfast and get the seven-forty train? Quarter of six by the latest, and *you* must get up earlier than that, because you're at the hotel and have further to go. Come here for breakfast, and—listen—be here by half-past six—are you *listening*, Condy?—and we'll go down to the depot from here. Don't forget to bring the rods."

"I'll wear my bicycle suit," he said, "and one of those golf scarfs that wrap around your neck."

"No," she declared, "I won't have it. Wear the oldest clothes you've got, but look fairly respectable, because we're to go to Luna's when we get back, remember. And now go home; you need all the sleep you can get if you are to get up at six o'clock."

Instead of being late, as Blix had feared, Conde was absurdly ahead of time the next morning. For a wonder, he had not forgotten the rods; but he was one tremor of nervousness. He would eat no breakfast.

"We're going to miss that train," he would announce from time to time; "I just know it. Blix, look what time it is. We ought to be on the way to the depot now. Come on; you don't want any more coffee. Have you got everything? Did you put the reels in the lunch-basket?—and the fly-book? Lord, if we should forget the fly-book!"

He managed to get her to the depot over half an hour ahead of time. The train had not even backed in, nor the ticket office opened.

"I told you, Conde, I told you," complained Blix, sinking helplessly upon a bench in the waiting-room.

"No—no—no," he answered vaguely, looking nervously about, his head in the air. "We're none too soon—have more time to rest now. I wonder what track the train leaves from. I wonder if it stops at San Bruno. I wonder how far it is from San Bruno to Lake San Andreas. I'm afraid it's going to rain. Heavens and earth, Blix, we forgot the shrimps!"

"No, *no*! Sit down, I've got the shrimps. Conde, you make me so nervous I shall scream in a minute."

Some three-quarters of an hour later the train had set them down at San Bruno—nothing more than a roadhouse, the headquarters for duck-shooters and fishermen from the city. However, Blix and Conde were the only visitors. Everybody seemed to be especially nice to them on that wonderful morning. Even the supercilious ticket-seller at the San Francisco depot had unbent, and wished them good luck. The conductor of the train had shown himself affable. The very brakeman had gone out of his way to apprise them, quite five minutes ahead of time, that "the next stop was their place." And at San Bruno the proprietor of the roadhouse himself hitched up to drive them over to the lake, announcing that he would call for them at "Richardson's" in time for the evening train.

"And he only asked me four bits for both trips," whispered Conde to Blix as they jogged along.

The country was beautiful. It was hardly eight o'clock, and the morning still retained much of the brisk effervescence of the early dawn. Great bare, rolling hills of gray-green, thinly scattered with live-oak, bore back from the road on either hand. The sky was pale blue. There was a smell of cows in the air, and twice they heard an unseen lark singing. It was very still. The old buggy and complacent horse were embalmed in a pungent aroma of old leather and of stables that was entrancing; and a sweet smell of grass and sap came to them in occasional long whiffs. There was exhilaration in the very thought of being alive on that odorous, still morning. The young blood went spanking in the veins. Blix's cheeks were ruddy, her little dark-brown eyes fairly coruscating with pleasure.

"Conde, isn't it all splendid?" she suddenly burst out.

"I feel regularly bigger," he declared solemnly. "I could do anything a morning like this."

Then they came to the lake, and to Richardson's, where the farmer lived who was also the custodian of the lake. The complacent horse jogged back, and Conde and Blix set about the serious business of the day. Conde had no need to show Richardson the delightful sporting clerk's card. The old Yankee—his twang and dry humor singularly incongruous on that royal morning—was solicitude itself. He picked out the best boat on the beach for them, loaned them his own anchor of railroad iron, indicated minutely the point on the opposite shore off which the last big trout had been "killed," and wetted himself to his ankles as he pushed off the boat.

Conde took the oars. Blix sat in the stern, jointing the rods and running the lines through the guides. She even baited the hooks with the salt shrimp herself, and by nine o'clock they were at anchor some forty feet off shore, and fishing, according to Richardson's advice, "a leetle mite off the edge o' the weeds."

"If we don't get a bite the whole blessed day," said Conde, as he paid out his line to the ratchet music of the reel, "we'll have fun just the same. Look around—isn't this great?"

They were absolutely alone. The day was young yet. The lake, smooth and still as gray silk, widened to the west and south without so much as a wrinkle to roughen the surface. Only to the east, where the sun looked over a shoulder of a higher hill, it flamed up into a blinding diamond iridescence. The surrounding land lay between sky and water, hushed to a Sunday stillness. Far off across the lake by Richardson's they heard a dog bark, and the sound came fine and small and delicate. At long intervals the boat stirred with a gentle clap-clapping of the water along its sides. From the nearby shore in the growth of manzanita bushes quail called and clucked comfortably to each other; a bewildered yellow butterfly danced by over their heads, and slim blue dragonflies came and poised on their lines and fishing-rods, bowing their backs.

From his seat in the bow, Conde cast a glance at Blix. She was holding her rod in both hands, absorbed, watchful, very intent. She was as trim as ever, even in the old clothes she had worn for the occasion. Her round, strong neck was as usual swathed high and tight in white, and the huge dog-collar girdled her waist according to her custom. She had taken off her hat. Her yellow hair rolled back from her round forehead and cool pink cheeks like a veritable nimbus, and for the fiftieth time Conde remarked the charming contrast of her small, deep-brown eyes in the midst of this white satin, yellow hair, white skin, and exquisite pink cheeks.

An hour passed. Then two.

"No fish," murmured Conde, drawing in his line to examine the bait. But, as he was fumbling with the flies he was startled by a sharp exclamation from Blix.

"Oh! Condy—I've got a bite!"

He looked up just in time to see the tip of her rod twitch, twitch, twitch. Then the whole rod arched suddenly, the reel sang, the line tautened and cut diagonally through the water.

"You got him! You got him!" he shouted, palpitating with excitement. "And he's a good one!"

Blix rose, reeling in as rapidly as was possible, the butt of the twitching, living rod braced against her belt. All at once the rod straightened out again, the strain was released, and the line began to slant rapidly away from the boat.

"He's off!" she cried.

"Off, nothing! *He's going to jump.* Look out for him, now!"

And then the two watching from the boat, tense and quivering with the drama of the moment, saw that most inspiriting of sights—the "break" of a salmon-trout. Up he went, from a brusque explosion of ripples and foam—up into the gray of the morning from out the gray of the water: scales all gleaming, hackles all a-bristle; a sudden flash of silver, a sweep as of a scimitar in gray smoke, with a splash, a turmoil, an abrupt burst of troubled sound that stabbed through the silence of the morning, and in a single instant dissipated all the placid calm of the previous hours.

"Keep the line taut," whispered Conde, gritting his teeth. "When he comes toward you, reel him in; an' if he pulls too hard, give him his head."

Blix was breathing fast, her cheeks blazing, her eyes all alight.

"Oh," she gasped, "I'm so afraid I'll lose him! Oh, look at that!" she cried, as the trout darted straight for the bottom, bending the rod till the tip was submerged. "Conde, I'll lose him—I know I shall; you, *you* take the rod!"

"Not for a thousand dollars! Steady, there, he's away again! Oh, talk about *sport*!"

Yard by yard Blix reeled in until they began to see the silver glint of the trout's flanks through the green water. She brought him nearer. Swimming parallel with the boat, he was plainly visible from his wide-opened mouth—the hook and fly protruding from his lower jaw—to the red, quivering flanges of the tail. His sides were faintly speckled, his belly white as chalk. He was almost as long as Condy's forearm.

"Oh, he's a beauty! Oh, isn't he a beauty!" murmured Conde. "Now, careful, careful; bring him up to the boat where I can reach him; easy, Blix. If he bolts again, let him run."

Twice the trout shied from the boat's shadow, and twice, as Blix gave him his head, the reel sang and hummed like a watchman's rattle. But the third time he came to the surface and turned slowly on his side, the white belly and one red fin out of the water, the gills opening and shutting. He was tired out. A third time Blix drew him gently to the boat's side. Conde reached out and down into the water till his very shoulder was wet, hooked two fingers under the distended gills, and with a long, easy movement of the arm swung him into the boat.

Their exultation was that of veritable children. Conde whooped like an Apache, throwing his hat into the air; Blix was hardly articulate, her hands clasped, her hair in disarray, her eyes swimming with tears of sheer excitement. They shook each other's hands; they talked wildly at the same time: they pounded on the boat's thwarts with their fists; they laughed at their own absurdity; they looked at the trout again and again, guessed at his weight, and recalled to each other details of the struggle.

"When he broke that time, wasn't it grand?"

"And when I first felt him bite! It was so sudden—why, it actually frightened me. I never—no, never in my life!" exclaimed Blix, "was so happy as I am at this moment. Oh, Conde, to think—just to *think*!"

"Isn't it glory hallelujah?"

"Isn't it better than teas, and dancing, and functions?"

"Blix—how old are we?"

"I don't care how old we are; I think that trout will weigh two pounds."

When they were calm again, they returned to their fishing. The morning passed, and it was noon before they were aware of it. By half-past twelve Blix had caught three trout, though the first was by far the heaviest. Conde had not had so much as a bite. At one o'clock they rowed ashore and had lunch under a huge live-oak in a little amphitheater of manzanita.

Never had a lunch tasted so delicious. What if the wine was warm and the stuffed olives oily? What if the pepper for the hard-boiled eggs had sifted all over the "devilish" ham sandwiches? What if the eggs themselves had not been sufficiently cooked, and the corkscrew forgotten? They *could* not be anything else but inordinately happy, sublimely gay. Nothing short of actual tragedy could have marred the joy of that day.

But after they were done eating, and Blix had put away the forks and spoons, and while Conde was stretched upon his back smoking a cigar, she said to him:

"Now, Conde, what do you say to a little game of cards with me?"

The cigar dropped from Condy's lips, and he sat suddenly upright, brushing the fallen leaves from his hair. Blix had taken a deck of cards from the lunch-basket, and four rolls of chips wrapped in tissue paper. He stared at her in speechless amazement.

"What do you say?" she repeated, looking at him and smiling.

"Why, Blix!" he exclaimed in amazement, "what do you mean?"

"Just what I say. I want you to play cards with me."

"I'll not to do it," he declared, almost coldly.

"Listen to me, Conde," answered Blix; and for quite five minutes, while he interrupted and protested and pshawed and argued, she talked to him calmly and quietly.

"I don't ask you to stop playing, Conde," she said, as she finished. "I just ask you that when you feel you must play—or—I mean, when you want to very bad, you will come and play with me, instead of playing at your club."

"But it's absurd, it's preposterous. I hate to see a girl gambling—and you of all girls!"

"It's no worse for me than it is for you and—well, do you suppose I would play with any one else? Maybe you think I can't play well enough to make it interesting for you," she said gayly. "Is that it? I can soon show you, Conde Rivers—never mind when I learned how."

"But, Blix, you don't know how often we play, those men and I. Why, it is almost every—you don't know how often we play."

"Conde, whenever you want to play, and will play with ME, no matter what I've got in hand, I'll stop everything and play with you."

"But why?"

"Because I think, Conde, that *this* way perhaps you won't play quite so often at first; and then little by little perhaps—perhaps—well, never mind that now. I want to play; put it that way. But I want you to promise me never to play with any one else—say for six months."

And in the end, whipped by a sense of shame, Conde made her the promise. They became very gay upon the instant.

"Hoh!" exclaimed Conde; "what do *you* know of poker? I think we had best play old sledge or cassino."

Blix had dealt a hand and partitioned the chips.

"Straights and flushes *before* the draw," she announced calmly.

Conde started and stared; then, looking at her askance, picked up his hand.

"It's up to you."

"I'll make it five to play."

"Five? Very well. How many cards?"

"Three."

"I'll take two."

"Bet you five more."

Blix looked at her hand. Then, without trace of expression in her voice or face, said:

"There's your five, and I ll raise you five."

"Five better."

"And five better than that."

"Call you."

"Full house. Aces on tens," said Blix, throwing down her cards.

"Heavens! They're good as gold," muttered Conde as Blix gathered in the chips.

An hour later she had won all the chips but five.

"Now we'll stop and get to fishing again; don't you want to?"

He agreed, and she counted the chips.

"Conde, you owe me seven dollars and a half," she announced.

Conde began to smile. "Well," he said jocosely, "I'll send you around a check tomorrow."

But at this Blix was cross upon the instant. "You wouldn't do that— wouldn't talk that way with one of your friends at the club!" she exclaimed; "and it's not right to do it with me. Conde, give me seven dollars and a half. When you play cards with me it's just as though it were with another man. I would have paid you if you had won."

"But I haven't got more than nine dollars. Who'll pay for the supper tonight at Luna's, and our railroad fare going home?"

"I'll pay."

"But I—I can't afford to lose money this way."

"Shouldn't have played, then. I took the same chances as you. Conde, I want my money."

"You—you—why you've regularly flimflammed me."

"Will you give me my money?"

"Oh, take your money then!"

Blix shut the money in her purse, and rose, dusting her dress.

"Now," she said, "now that the pastime of card-playing is over, we will return to the serious business of life, which is the catching—no, '_killing_' of lake trout."

At five o'clock in the afternoon, Conde pulled up the anchor of railroad iron and rowed back to Richardson's. Blix had six trout to her credit, but Condy's ill-luck had been actually ludicrous.

"I can hold a string in the water as long as anybody," he complained, "but I'd like to have the satisfaction of merely changing the bait *occasionally*. I've not had a single bite—not a nibble, y' know, all day. Never mind, you got the big trout, Blix; that first one. That five minutes was worth the whole day. It's been glorious, the whole thing. We'll come down here once a week right along now."

But the one incident that completed the happiness of that wonderful day occurred just as they were getting out of the boat on the shore by Richardson's. In a mud-hole between two rocks they discovered a tiny striped snake, hardly bigger than a lead pencil, in the act of swallowing a little green frog, and they passed a rapt ten minutes in witnessing the progress of this miniature drama, which culminated happily in the victim's escape, and triumph of virtue.

"That," declared Blix as they climbed into the old buggy which was to take them to the train, "was the one thing necessary. That made the day perfect."

They reached the city at dusk, and sent their fish, lunch-basket, and rods up to the Bessemers' flat by a messenger boy with an explanatory note for Blix's father.

"Now," said Conde, "for Luna's and the matrimonial objects."

Chapter VII

Luna's Mexican restaurant has no address. It is on no particular street, at no particular corner; even its habitues, its most enthusiastic devotees, are unable to locate it upon demand. It is "over there in the quarter," "not far from the cathedral there." One could find it if one started out with that intent; but to direct another there—no, that is out of the question. It *can* be reached by following the alleys of Chinatown. You will come out of the last alley—the one where the slave girls are—upon the edge of the Mexican quarter, and by going straight forward a block or two and by keeping a sharp lookout to right and left you will hit upon it. It is always to be searched for. Always to be discovered.

On that particular Monday evening Blix and Conde arrived at Luna's some fifteen minutes before seven. Conde had lost himself and all sense of direction in the strange streets of the quarter, and they were on the very brink of despair when Blix discovered the sign upon an opposite corner.

As Conde had foretold, they had the place to themselves. They went into the back room with its one mirror, six tables, and astonishing curtains of Nottingham lace; and the waiter, whose name was Richard or Riccardo, according to taste, began to officiate at the solemn rites of the "supper Mexican." Conde and Blix ate with their eyes continually wandering to the door; and as the *frijoles* were being served, started simultaneously and exchanged glances.

A man wearing two marguerites in the lapel of his coat had entered abruptly, and sat down to a table close at hand.

Conde drew a breath of suppressed excitement.

"There he is," he whispered—"Captain Jack!"

They looked at the newcomer with furtive anxiety, and told themselves that they were disappointed. For a retired sea captain he was desperately commonplace. His hair was red, he was younger than they had expected, and, worst of all, he did look tough.

"Oh, poor K. D. B.!" sighed Blix, shaking her head. "He'll never do, I'm afraid. Perhaps he has a good heart, though; red-headed people are *sometimes* affectionate."

"They are impulsive," hazarded Conde.

As he spoke the words, a second man entered the little room. He, too, sat down at a nearby table. He, too, ordered the "supper Mexican." He, too, wore marguerites in his buttonhole.

"Death and destruction!" gasped Conde, turning pale.

Blix collapsed helplessly in her chair, her hands dropping in her lap. They stared at each other in utter confusion.

"Here's a how-do-you-do," murmured Conde, pretending to strip a *tamale* that Richard had just set before him. But Blix had pushed hers aside.

"What does it mean?" whispered Conde across the table. "In Heaven's name, what does it mean?"

"It can only mean one thing," Blix declared; "one of them is the captain, and one is a coincidence. Anybody might wear a marguerite; we ought to have thought of that."

"But which is which?"

"If K. D. B. should come now!"

"But the last man looks more like the captain."

The last man was a sturdy, broad-shouldered fellow, who might have been forty. His heavy mustache was just touched with gray, and he did have a certain vaguely "sober and industrious" appearance. But the difference between the two men was slight, after all; the red-headed man could easily have been a sea captain, and he certainly was over thirty-five.

"Which? which? which?—how can we tell? We might think of some way to get rid of the coincidence, if we could only tell which the coincidence was. We owe it to K. D. B. In a way, Conde, it's our duty. We brought her here, or we are going to, and we ought to help her all we can; and she may be here at any moment. What time is it now?"

"Five minutes after seven. But, Blix, I should think the right one—the captain—would be all put out himself by seeing another chap here wearing marguerites. Does either one of 'em seem put out to you? Look. I should think the captain, whichever one he is, would kind of *glare* at the coincidence."

Stealthily they studied the two men for a moment.

"No, no," murmured Blix, "you can't tell. Neither of them seems to glare much. Oh, Condy"—her voice dropped to a faint whisper. "The red-headed one has put his hat on a chair, just behind him, notice? Do you suppose if you stood up you could see inside?"

"What good would that do?"

"He might have his initials inside the crown, or his whole name even; and you could see if he had a 'captain' before it."

Conde made a pretense of rising to get a match in a ribbed, truncated cone of china that stood upon an adjacent table, and Blix held her breath as he glanced down into the depths of the hat. He resumed his seat.

"Only initials," he breathed. "W. J. A. It might be Jack, that J., and it might be Joe, or Jeremiah, or Joshua; and even if he was a captain he might not use the title. We're no better off than we were before."

"And K. D. B. may come at any moment. Maybe she has come already and looked through the windows, and saw *two* men with marguerites and went away. She'd be just that timid. What can we do?"

"Wait a minute, look here," murmured Conde. "I've an idea. *I'll* find out which the captain is. You see that picture, that chromo, on the wall opposite?"

Blix looked as he indicated. The picture was a gorgeously colored lithograph of a pilot-boat, schooner-rigged, all sails set, dashing bravely through seas of emerald green color.

"You mean that schooner?" asked Blix.

"That schooner, exactly. Now, listen. You ask me in a loud voice what kind of a boat that is; and when I answer, you keep your eye on the two men."

"Why, what are you going to do?"

"You'll see. Try it now; we've no time to lose."

Blix shifted in her seat and cleared her throat. Then:

"What a pretty boat that is up there, that picture on the wall. See over there, on the wall opposite? Do you notice it? Isn't she pretty? Conde, tell me what kind of a boat is that?"

Conde turned about in his place with great deliberation, fixed the picture with a judicial eye, and announced decisively:

"That?—why, that's a *Barkentine*."

Conde had no need to wait for Blix's report. The demonstration came far too quickly for that. The red-headed man at his loud declaration merely glanced in the direction of the chromo and returned to his *enchellados*. But he of the black mustache followed Condy's glance, noted the picture of which he spoke, and snorted contemptuously. They even heard him mutter beneath his mustache:

"*Barkentine* your eye!"

"No doubt as to which is the captain now," whispered Conde so soon as the other had removed from him a glance of withering scorn.

They could hardly restrain their gaiety; but their gravity promptly returned when Blix kicked Condy's foot under the table and murmured: "He's looking at his watch, the captain is. K. D. B. isn't here yet, and the red-headed man, the coincidence, is. We *must* get rid of him. Conde, can't you think of something?"

"Well, he won't go till he's through his supper, you can depend upon that. If he's here when K. D. B. arrives, it will spoil everything. She wouldn't stay a moment. She wouldn't even come in."

"Isn't it disappointing? And I had so counted upon bringing these two together! And Captain Jack is a nice man!"

"You can see that with one hand tied behind you," whispered Conde. "The other chap's tough."

"Looks just like the kind of man to get into jail sooner or later."

"Maybe he's into some mischief now; you never can tell. And the Mexican quarter of San Francisco is just the place for 'affairs.' I'll warrant he's got *pals.*"

"Well, here he is—that's the main point—just keeping those people apart, spoiling a whole romance. Maybe ruining their lives. It's *quite* possible; really it is. Just stop and think. This is a positive crisis we're looking at now."

"Can't we get rid of him *somehow?*"

"O-oh!" whispered Blix, all at once, in a quiver of excitement. "There is a way, if we'd ever have the courage to do it. It might work; and if it didn't, he'd never know the difference, never would suspect us. Oh! But we wouldn't dare."

"What? what? In Heaven's name what is it, Blix?"

"We wouldn't dare—we couldn't. Oh! But it would be such—"

"K. D. B. may come in that door at any second."

"I'm half afraid, but all the same—Conde, let me have a pencil." She dashed off a couple of lines on the back of the bill of fare, and her hand trembled like a leaf as she handed him what she had written.

"Send him—the red-headed man—that telegram. There's an office just two doors below here, next the drugstore. I saw it as we came by. You know his initials: remember, you saw them in his hat. W. J. A., Luna's restaurant. That's all you want."

"Lord," muttered Conde, as he gazed upon what Blix had written.

"Do you dare?" she whispered, with a little hysterical shudder.

"If it failed we've nothing to lose."

"And K. D. B. is coming nearer every instant!"

"But would he go—that is, at once?"

"We can only try. You won't be gone a hundred seconds. You can leave me here that length of time. Quick, Conde; decide one way or the other. It's getting desperate."

Conde reached for his hat.

"Give me some money, then," he said. "You won all of mine."

A few moments later he was back again and the two sat, pretending to eat their chili peppers, their hearts in their throats, hardly daring to raise their eyes from their plates. Conde was actually sick with excitement, and all but tipped the seltzer bottle to the floor when a messenger boy appeared in the outer room. The boy and the proprietor held a conference over the counter. Then Richard appeared between the portieres of Nottingham lace, the telegram in his hand and the boy at his heels.

Evidently Richard knew the red-headed man, for he crossed over to him at once with the words:

"I guess this is for you, Mr. Atkins?"

He handed him the despatch and retired. The red-headed man signed the receipt; the boy departed. Blix and Conde heard the sound of torn paper as the red-headed man opened the telegram.

Ten seconds passed, then fifteen, then twenty. There was a silence. Conde dared to steal a glance at the red-headed man's reflection in the mirror. He was studying the despatch, frowning horribly. He put it away in his pocket, took it out again with a fierce movement of impatience, and consulted it a second time. His "supper Mexican" remained untasted before him; Conde and Blix heard him breathing loud through his nose. That he was profoundly agitated, they could not doubt for a single moment. All at once a little panic terror seemed to take possession of him. He rose, seized his hat, jammed it over his ears, slapped a half-dollar upon the table, and strode from the restaurant.

This is what the read-headed man had read in the despatch; this is what Blix had written:

All is discovered. Fly at once.

And never in all their subsequent rambles about the city did Blix or Conde set eyes upon the red-headed man again, nor did Luna's restaurant, where he seemed to have been a habitue, ever afterward know his presence. He disappeared; he was swallowed up. He had left the restaurant, true. Had he also left that neighborhood? Had he fled the city, the State, the country even? What skeleton in the red-headed man's closet had those six words called to life and the light of day. Had they frightened him forth to spend the rest of his days fleeing from an unnamed, unknown avenger—a veritable wandering Jew? What mystery had they touched upon there in the bald, bare back room of the Quarter's restaurant? What dark door had they opened, what red-headed phantom had they evoked? Had they broken up a plot, thwarted a conspiracy, prevented a crime? They never knew. One thing only was certain. The red-headed man had had a past.

Meanwhile the minutes were passing, and K. D. B. still failed to appear. Captain Jack was visibly growing impatient, anxious. By now he had come to the fiery liqueur called mescal. He was nearly through his supper. At every moment he consulted his watch and fixed the outside door with a scowl. It was already twenty minutes after seven.

"I know the red-headed man spoiled it, after all," murmured Blix. "K. D. B. saw the two of them in here and was frightened."

"We could send Captain Jack a telegram from her," suggested Conde. "I'm ready for anything now."

"What could you say?"

"Oh, that she couldn't come. Make another appointment."

"He'd be offended with her. He'd never make another appointment. Sea captains are always so punctilious, y' know."

Richard brought them their coffee and kirsch, and Conde showed Blix how to burn a lump of sugar and sweeten the coffee with syrup. But they were disappointed. Captain Jack was getting ready to leave. K. D. B. had evidently broken the appointment.

Then all at once she appeared.

They knew it upon the instant by a brisk opening and shutting of the street door, and by a sudden alertness on the part of Captain Jack, which he immediately followed by a quite inexplicable move. The street door in the outside room had hardly closed before his hand shot to his coat lapel and tore out the two marguerites.

The action was instinctive; Blix knew it for such immediately. The retired captain had not premeditated it. He had not seen the face of the newcomer. She had not time to come into the back room, or even to close the street door. But the instant that the captain had recognized a bunch of white marguerites in her belt he had, without knowing why, been moved to conceal his identity.

"He's afraid," whispered Blix. "Positively, I believe he's afraid. How absolutely stupid men are!"

But meanwhile, K. D. B., the looked-for, the planned-for and intrigued-for; the object of so much diplomacy, such delicate maneuvering; the pivot upon which all plans were to turn, the storm-center round which so many conflicting currents revolved, and for whose benefit the peace of mind of the red-headed man had been forever broken up—had entered the room.

"Why, she's *pretty!*" was Blix's first smothered exclamation, as if she had expected a harridan.

K. D. B. looked like a servant-girl of the better sort, and was really very neatly dressed. She was small, little even. She had snappy black eyes, a resolute mouth, and a general air of being very quiet, very matter-of-fact and complacent. She would be disturbed at nothing, excited at nothing; Blix was sure of that. She was placid, but it was the placidity not of the absence of emotion, but of emotion disdained. Not the placidity of the mollusk, but that of a mature and contemplative cat.

Quietly she sat down at a corner table, quietly she removed her veil and gloves, and quietly she took in the room and its three occupants.

Conde and Blix glued their eyes upon their coffee cups like guilty conspirators; but a crash of falling crockery called their attention to the captain's table.

Captain Jack was in a tremor. Hitherto he had acted the role of a sane and sensible gentleman of middle age, master of himself and of the situation. The entrance of K. D. B. had evidently reduced him to a semi-idiotic condition. He enlarged himself; he eased his neck in his collar with a rotary movement of head and shoulders. He frowned terribly at trifling objects in corners of the room. He cleared his throat till the glassware jingled. He pulled at his mustache. He perspired, fumed, fretted, and was suddenly seized with an insane desire to laugh. Once only he caught the eye of K. D. B., calmly sitting in her corner, picking daintily at her fish, whereupon he immediately overturned the vinegar and pepper casters upon the floor. Just so might have behaved an overgrown puppy in the presence of a sleepy, unperturbed chessy-cat, dozing by the fire.

"He ought to be shaken," murmured Blix at the end of her patience. "Does he think *she* is going to make the first move?"

"Ha, ah'm!" thundered the captain, clearing his throat for the twentieth time, twirling his mustache, and burying his scarlet face in an enormous pocket handkerchief.

Five minutes passed and he was still in his place. From time to time K. D. B. fixed him with a quiet, deliberate look, and resumed her delicate picking.

"Do you think she knows it's he, now that he's taken off his marguerites?" whispered Conde.

"Know it?—of course she does! Do you think women are absolutely *blind*, or so imbecile as men are? And, then, if she didn't think it was he, she'd go away. And she's so really pretty, too. He ought to thank his stars alive. Think what a fright she might have been! She doesn't *look* thirty-one."

"Huh!" returned Conde. "As long as she *said* she was thirty-one, you can bet everything you have that she is; that's as true as revealed religion."

"Well, it's something to have seen the kind of people who write the personals," said Blix. "I had always imagined that they were kind of tough."

"You see they are not," he answered. "I told you they were not. Maybe, however, we have been exceptionally fortunate. At any rate, these are respectable enough."

"Not the least doubt about that. But why don't he do something, that captain?" mourned Blix. "Why *will* he act like such a ninny?"

"He's waiting for us to go," said Conde; "I'm sure of it. They'll never meet so long as we're here. Let's go and give 'em a chance. If you leave the two alone here, one or the other will *have* to speak. The suspense would become too terrible. It would be as though they were on a desert island."

"But I wanted to *see* them meet," she protested.

"You wouldn't hear what they said."

"But we'd never know if they did meet, and oh—and *who* spoke first?"

"She'll speak first," declared Conde.

"Never!" returned Blix, in an indignant whisper.

"I tell you what. We could go and then come back in five minutes. I'll forget my stick here. Savvy?"

"You would probably do it anyhow," she told him.

They decided this would be the better course. They got together their things, and Conde neglected his stick, hanging upon a hook on the wall.

At the counter in the outside room, Blix, to the stupefaction of Richard, the waiter, paid the bill. But as she was moving toward the door, Conde called her back.

"Remember the waiter," he said severely, while Richard grinned and bobbed. "Fifty cents is the very least you could tip him." Richard actually protested, but Conde was firm, and insisted upon a half-dollar tip.

"Noblesse oblige," he declared with vast solemnity.

They walked as far as the cathedral, listened for a moment to the bell striking the hour of eight; then as they remembered that the restaurant closed at that time, hurried back and entered the outside room in feigned perturbation.

"Did I, could I have possibly left my stick here?" exclaimed Conde to Richard, who was untying his apron behind the counter. But Richard had not noticed.

"I think I must have left it back here where we were sitting."

Conde stepped into the back room, Blix following. They got his stick and returned to the outside room.

"Yes, yes, I did leave it," he said, as he showed it to Richard. "I'm always leaving that stick wherever I go."

"Come again," said Richard, as he bowed them out of the door.

On the curb outside Conde and Blix shook hands and congratulated each other on the success of all their labors. In the back room, seated at the same table, a bunch of wilting marguerites between them, they had seen their "matrimonial objects" conferring earnestly together, absorbed in the business of getting acquainted.

Blix heaved a great sigh of relief and satisfaction, exclaiming:

"At last K. D. B. and Captain Jack have met!"

Chapter VIII

"But," she added, as they started to walk, "we will never know which one spoke first."

But Conde was already worrying.

"I don't know, I don't know!" he murmured anxiously. "Perhaps we've done an awful thing. Suppose they aren't happy together after they're married? I wish we hadn't; I wish we hadn't now. We've been playing a game of checkers with human souls. We've an awful responsibility. Suppose he kills her some time?"

"Fiddlesticks, Conde! And, besides, if we've done wrong with our matrimonial objects, we've offset it by doing well with our red-headed coincidence. How do you know, you may have 'foiled a villain' with that telegram—prevented a crime?"

Conde grinned at the recollection of the incident.

"'Fly at once,'" he repeated. "I guess he's flying yet. 'All is discovered.' I'd give a dollar and a half—"

"If you had it?"

"Oh, well, if I had it—to know just what it was we have discovered."

Suddenly Blix caught his arm.

"Conde, here they come!"

"Who? Who?"

"Our objects, Captain Jack and K. D. B."

"Of course, of course. They couldn't stay. The restaurant shuts up at eight."

Blix and Conde had been walking slowly in the direction of Pacific Street, and K. D. B. and her escort soon overtook them going in the same direction. As they passed, the captain was saying:

"—jumped on my hatches, and says we'll make it an international affair. That didn't—"

A passing wagon drowned the sound of his voice.

"He was telling her of his adventures!" cried Blix. "Splendid! Othello and Desdemona. They're getting on."

"Let's follow them!" exclaimed Conde.

"Should we? Wouldn't it be indiscreet?"

"No. We are the arbiters of their fate; we *must* take an interest."

They allowed their objects to get ahead some half a block and then fell in behind. There was little danger of their being detected. The captain and K. D. B. were absorbed in each other. She had even taken his arm.

"They make a fine-looking couple, really," said Blix. "Where do you suppose they are going? To another restaurant?"

But this was not the case. Blix and Conde followed them as far as Washington Square, where the Geodetic Survey stone stands, and the enormous flagstaff; and there in front of a commonplace little house, two doors above the Russian church with its minarets like inverted balloons K. D. B. and the captain halted. For a few moments they conversed in low tones at the gate, then said good-night, K. D. B. entering the house, the captain bowing with great deference, his hat in his hand. Then he turned about, glanced once or twice at the house, set his hat at an angle, and disappeared across the square, whistling a tune, his chin in the air.

"Very good, excellent, highly respectable," approved Blix; and Conde himself fetched a sigh of relief.

"Yes, yes, it might have been worse."

"We'll never see them again, our 'Matrimonial Objects,'" said Blix, "and they'll never know about us; but we have brought them together. We've started a romance. Yes, I think we've done a good day's work. And now, Conde, I think we had best be thinking of home ourselves. I'm just beginning to get most awfully sleepy. What a day we've had!"

A sea fog, or rather *the* sea fog—San Francisco's old and inseparable companion—had gathered by the time they reached the top of the Washington Street hill. Everything was wet with it. The asphalt was like varnished ebony. Indistinct masses and huge dim shadows stood for the houses on either side. From the eucalyptus trees and the palms the water dripped like rain. Far off oceanward, the fog-horn was lowing like a lost gigantic bull. The gray bulk of a policeman—the light from the street lamp reflected in his star—loomed up on the corner as they descended from the car.

*   *   *

Conde had intended to call his diver's story *A Submarine Romance*, but Blix had disapproved.

"It's too *Twenty Thousand Leagues Under the Sea*," she had said. "You want something much more dignified. There is that about you, Conde, you like to be too showy; you don't know when to stop. But you have left off red-and-white scarfs, and I am very glad to see you wearing white shirtfronts instead of pink ones."

"Yes, yes, I thought it would be quieter," he had answered, as though the idea had come from him. Blix allowed him to think so.

But *A Victory Over Death*, as the story was finally called, was a success.

Conde was too much of a born storyteller not to know when he had done something distinctly good. When the story came back from the typewriter's, with the additional strength that print lends to fiction, and he had read it over, he could not repress a sense of jubilation. The story rang true.

"Bully, bully!" he muttered between his teeth as he finished the last paragraph. "It's a corker! If it's rejected everywhere, it's an out-of-sight yarn just the same."

And there Condy's enthusiasm in the matter began to dwindle. The fine fire which had sustained him during the story s composition had died out. He was satisfied with his work. He had written a good story, and that was the end of it. No doubt he would send it East—to the Centennial Company—tomorrow or the day after—some time that week. To mail the manuscript meant quite half an hour's effort. He would have to buy stamps for return postage; a letter would have to be written, a large envelope procured, the accurate address ascertained. For the moment his supplement work demanded his attention. He put off sending the story from day to day. His interest in it had abated. And for that matter he soon discovered he had other things to think of.

It had been easy to promise Blix that he would no longer gamble at his club with the other men of his acquaintance; but it was "death and the devil," as he told himself, to abide by that promise. More than once in the fortnight following upon his resolution he had come up to the little flat on the Washington Street hill as to a place of refuge; and Blix, always pretending that it was all a huge joke and part of their good times, had brought out the cards and played with him. But she knew very well the fight he was making against the enemy, and how hard it was for him to keep from the round green tables and group of silent shirt-sleeved men in the card-rooms of his club. She looked forward to the time when Conde would cease to play even with her. But she was too sensible and practical a girl to expect him to break a habit of years' standing in a couple of weeks. The thing would have to be accomplished little by little. At times she had misgivings as to the honesty of the course she had adopted. But nowadays, playing as he did with her only, Conde gambled but two or three evenings in the week, and then not for more than two hours at a time. Heretofore hardly an evening that had not seen him at the round table in his club's card-room, whence he had not risen until long after midnight.

Conde had told young Sargeant that he had "reformed" in the matter of gambling, and intended to swear off for a few months. Sargeant, like the thoroughbred he was, never urged him to play after that, and never spoke of the previous night's game when Conde was about. The other men of his "set" were no less thoughtful, and, though they rallied him a little at first upon his defection, soon let the matter drop. Conde told himself that there were plenty of good people in the world, after all. Every one seemed conspiring to make it easy for him, and he swore at himself for a weak-kneed cad.

On a certain Tuesday, about a week after the fishing excursion and the affair of the "Matrimonial Objects," toward half-past six in the evening, Conde was in his room, dressing for a dinner engagement. Young Sargeant's sister had invited him to be one of a party who were to dine at the University Club, and later on fill a box at a charity play, given by amateurs at one of the downtown theaters. But as he was washing his linen shirt-studs with his toothbrush his eye fell upon a note, in Laurie Flagg's handwriting, that lay on his writing-desk, and that he had received some ten days previous. Conde turned cold upon the instant, hurled the toothbrush across the room, and dropped into a chair with a groan of despair. Miss Flagg was giving a theater party for the same affair, and he remembered now that he had promised to join her party as well, forgetting all about the engagement he had made with Miss Sargeant. It was impossible at this late hour to accept either one of the young women's invitations without offending the other.

"Well, I won't go to *either*, that's all," he vociferated aloud to the opposite wall. "I'll send 'em each a wire, and say that I'm sick or have got to go down to the office, and—and, by George! I'll go up and see Blix, and we'll read and make things to eat."

And no sooner had this alternative occurred to him than it appeared too fascinating to be resisted. A weight seemed removed from his mind. When it came to that, what amusement would he have at either affair?

"Sit up there with your shirt-front starched like a board," he blustered, "and your collar throttling you, and smile till your face is sore, and reel off small talk to a girl whose last name you can't remember! Do I have any fun, does it do me any good, do I get ideas for yarns? What do I do it for? I don't know."

While speaking he had been kicking off his tight shoes and such of his full dress as he had already put on, and with a feeling of enormous relief turned again to his sack suit of tweed. "Lord, these feel better!" he exclaimed, as he substituted the loose business suit for the formal rigidity of his evening dress. It was with a sensation of positive luxury that he put on a "soft" shirt of blue cheviot and his tan walking-shoes.

"But no more red scarfs," he declared, as he knotted his black satin "club" before the mirror. "She *was* right there." He put his cigarettes in his pocket, caught up his gloves and stick, clapped on his hat, and started for the Bessemers' flat with a feeling of joyous expectancy he had not known for days.

Evidently Blix had seen him coming, for she opened the door herself; and it suited her humor for the moment to treat him as a peddler or book-agent.

"No, no," she said airily, her head in the air as she held the door. "No, we don't want any today. We *have* the biography of Abraham Lincoln. Don't want to subscribe to any *Home Book of Art*. We're not artistic; we use drapes in our parlors. Don't want *The Wives and Mothers of Great Men*."

But Conde had noticed a couple of young women on the lower steps of the adjacent flat, quite within earshot, and at once he began in a loud, harsh voice:

"Well, y' know, we can't wait for our rent forever; I'm only the collector, and I've nothing to do with repairs. Pay your rent that's three months overdue, and then—

But Blix pulled him within the house and clapped to the door.

"Conde *Rivers*!" she exclaimed, her cheeks flaming, "those are our neighbors. They heard every word. What do you suppose they think?"

"Huh! I'd rather have 'em think I was a rent-collector than a book-agent. You began it. Evenin', Miss Lady."

"Evenin', Mister Man."

But Condy's visit, begun thus gayly, soon developed along much more serious lines. After supper, while the light still lasted, Blix read stories to him while he smoked cigarettes in the bay window of the dining-room. But as soon as the light began to go she put the book aside, and the two took their accustomed places in the window, and watched the evening burning itself out over the Golden Gate.

It was just warm enough to have one of the windows opened, and for a long time after the dusk they sat listening to the vague clamor of the city, lapsing by degrees, till it settled into a measured, soothing murmur, like the breathing of some vast monster asleep. Condy's cigarette was a mere red point in the half-darkness. The smoke drifted out of the open window in long, blue strata. At his elbow Blix was leaning forward, looking down upon the darkening, drowsing city, her round, strong chin propped upon her hand. She was just close enough for Candy to catch the sweet, delicious feminine perfume that came indefinitely from her clothes, her hair, her neck. From where Conde sat he could see the silhouette of her head and shoulders against the dull golden blur of the open window; her round, high forehead, with the thick yellow hair rolling back from her temples and ears, her pink, clean cheeks, her little dark-brown, scintillating eyes, and her firm red mouth, made all the firmer by the position of her chin upon her hand. As ever, her round, strong neck was swathed high and tight in white satin; but between the topmost fold of the satin and the rose of one small earlobe was a little triangle of white skin, that was partly her neck and partly her cheek, and that Conde knew should be softer than down, smoother than satin, warm and sweet and redolent as new apples. Conde imagined himself having the right to lean toward her there and kiss that little spot upon her neck or her cheek; and as he fancied it, was surprised to find his breath come suddenly quick, and a barely perceptible qualm, as of a certain faintness, thrill him to his fingertips; and then, he thought, how would it be if he could, without fear of rebuff, reach out his arm and put it about her trim, firm waist, and draw her very close to him, till he should feel the satiny coolness of her smooth cheek against his; till he could sink his face in the delicious, fragrant confusion of her hair, then turn that face to his—that face with its strong, calm mouth and sweet, full lips—the face of this dear young girl of nineteen, and then—

"I say—I—shall we—let's read again. Let's—let's do something."

"Conde, how you frightened me!" exclaimed Blix, with a great start. "No, listen: I want to talk to you, to tell you something. Papum and I have been having some very long and serious talks since you were last here. What do you think, I may go away."

"The deuce you say!" exclaimed Conde, sitting suddenly upright. "Where to, in Heaven's name?" he added—"and when? and what for?"

"To New York, to study medicine."

There was a silence; then Conde exclaimed, waving his hands at her:

"Oh, go right on! Don't mind me. Little thing like going to New York—to study medicine. Of course, that happens every day, a mere detail. I presume you'll go back and forth for your meals?"

Then Blix began to explain. It appeared that she had two aunts, both sisters of her father—one a widow, the other unmarried. The widow, a certain Mrs. Kihm, lived in New York, and was wealthy, and had views on "women's sphere of usefulness." The other, Miss Bessemer, was a little old maid of fifty. Conde had on rare occasions seen at the flat, where everyone called her Aunt Dodd. She lived in that vague region of the city known as the Mission, where she owned a little property.

From what Blix told him that evening, Conde learned that Mrs. Kihm had visited the coast a few winters previous and had taken a great fancy to Blix. Even then she had proposed to Mr. Bessemer to take Blix back to New York with her, and educate her to some woman's profession; but at that time the old man would not listen to it. Now it seemed that the opportunity had again presented itself.

"She's a dear old lady," Blix said; "not a bit strong-minded, as you would think, and ever so much cleverer than most men. She manages all her property herself. For the last month she's been writing again to Papum for me to come on and stay with her three, or four years. She hasn't a chick nor a child, and she don't entertain or go out any, so maybe she feels lonesome. Of course if I studied there, Papum wouldn't think of Aunt Kihm— don't you know—paying for it all. I wouldn't go if it was that way. But I could stay with her and she could make a home for me while I was there—if I should study—anything—study medicine."

"But why!" he exclaimed. "What do you want to study to be a doctor for? It isn't as though you had to support yourself."

"I know, I know I've not got to support myself. But why shouldn't I have a profession just like a man—just like you, Conde? You stop and think. It seemed strange to me when I first thought of it; but I got thinking about it and talking it over with Papum, and I should LOVE it. I'd do it, not because I would have to do it, but because it would interest me. Conde, you know that I'm not a bit strong-minded, and that I hate a masculine, unfeminine girl as much as you do."

"But a medical college, Blix! You don't know what you are talking about."

"Yes, I do. There's a college in New York just for women. Aunt Kihm sent me the prospectus, and it's one of the best in the country. I don't dream of practicing, you know; at least, I don't think about that now. But one must have some occupation; and isn't studying medicine, Conde, better than piano-playing, or French courses, or literary classes and Browning circles? Oh, I've no patience with that kind of girl! And look at the chance I have now; and Aunt Kihm is such a dear! Think, she writes, I could go to and from the college in her coupe every day, and I would see New York; and just being in a big city like that is an education."

"You're right, it would be a big thing for you," assented Conde, "and I like the idea of you studying something. It would be the making of such a girl as you, Blix."

And then Blix, seeing him thus acquiescent, said:

"Well, it's all settled; Papum and I both wrote last night."

"When are you going?"

"The first week in January."

"Well, that's not so *awfully* soon. But who will take your place here? However in the world would your father get along without you—and Snooky and Howard?"

"Aunt Dodd is going to come."

"Sudden enough," said Conde, "but it *is* a great thing for you, Blix, and I'm mighty glad for you. Your future is all cut out for you now. Of course your aunt, if she's so fond of you and hasn't any children, will leave you everything—maybe settle something on you right away; and you'll marry one of those New York chaps, and be great big people before you know it."

"The idea, Conde!" she protested. "No; I'm going there to study medicine. Oh, you don't know how enthusiastic I am over the idea! I've bought some of the first-year books already, and have been reading them. Really, Conde, they are even better than *Many Inventions*."

"Wish I could get East," muttered Conde gloomily. Blix forgot her own good fortune upon the instant.

"I do so wish you *could*, Conde!" she exclaimed. "You are too good for a Sunday supplement. I know it and *you* know it, and I've heard ever so many people who have read your stories say the same thing. You could spend twenty years working as you are now, and at the end what would you be? Just an assistant editor of a Sunday supplement, and still in the same place; and worse, you'd come to be contented with that, and think you were only good for that and nothing better. You've got it in you, Conde, to be a great storyteller. I believe in you, and I've every confidence in you. But just so long as you stay here and are willing to do hack work, just so long you will be a hack writer. You must break from it; you *must* get away. I know you have a good time here; but there are so many things better than that and more worth while. You ought to make up your mind to get East, and work for that and nothing else. I know you want to go, but wanting isn't enough. Enthusiasm without energy isn't enough. You have enthusiasm, Conde; but you *must* have energy. You must be willing to give up things; you must make up your mind that you will go East, and then set your teeth together and do it. Oh, I *love* a man that can do that—make up his mind to a thing and then put it through!"

Conde watched her as she talked, her brown-black eyes coruscating, her cheeks glowing, her small hands curled into round pink fists.

"Blix, you're splendid!" he exclaimed; "you're fine! You could put life into a dead man. You're the kind of girl that are the making of men. By Jove, you'd back a man up, wouldn't you? You'd stand by him till the last ditch. Of course," he went on after a pause—"of course I ought to go to New York. But, Blix, suppose I went—well, then what? It isn't as though I had any income of my own, or rich aunt. Suppose I didn't find something to do—and the chances are that I wouldn't for three or four months—what would I live on in the meanwhile? 'What would the robin do then, poor thing?' I'm a poor young man, Miss Bessemer, and I've got to eat. No; my only chance is 'to be discovered' by a magazine or a publishing house or somebody, and get a bid of some kind."

"Well, there is the Centennial Company. They have taken an interest in you, Conde. You must follow that right up and keep your name before them all the time. Have you sent them *A Victory Over Death* yet?"

Conde sat down to his eggs and coffee the next morning in the hotel, harried with a certain sense of depression and disappointment for which he could assign no cause. Nothing seemed to interest him. The newspaper was dull. He could look forward to no pleasure in his day's work; and what was the matter with the sun that morning? As he walked down to the office he noted no cloud in the sky, but the brightness was gone from the day. He sat down to his desk and attacked his work, but "copy" would not come. The sporting editor and his inane jokes harassed him beyond expression. Just the sight of the clipping editor's back was an irritation. The office boy was a mere incentive to profanity. There was no spring in Conde that morning, no elasticity, none of his natural buoyancy. As the day wore on, his ennui increased; his luncheon at the club was tasteless, tobacco had lost its charm. He ordered a cocktail in the wine-room, and put it aside with a wry face.

The afternoon was one long tedium. At every hour he flung his pencil down, utterly unable to formulate the next sentence of his article, and, his hands in his pockets, gazed gloomily out of the window over the wilderness of roofs—grimy, dirty, ugly roofs that spread out below. He craved diversion, amusement, excitement. Something there was that he wanted with all his heart and soul; yet he was quite unable to say what it was. Something was gone from him today that he had possessed yesterday, and he knew he would not regain it on the morrow, nor the next day, nor the day after that. What was it? He could not say. For half an hour he imagined he was going to be sick. His mother was not to be at home that evening, and Conde dined at his club in the hopes of finding someone with whom he could go to the theater later on in the evening. Sargeant joined him over his coffee and cigarette, but declined to go with him to the theater.

"Another game on tonight?" asked Conde.

"I suppose so," admitted the other.

"I guess I'll join you tonight," said Conde. "I've had the blue devils since morning, and I've got to have something to drive them off."

"Don't let me urge you, you know," returned Sargeant.

"Oh, that's all right!" Conde assured him. "My time's about up, any-ways."

An hour later, just as he, Sargeant, and the other men of their "set" were in the act of going upstairs to the card-rooms, a hall-boy gave Conde a note, at that moment brought by a messenger, who was waiting for an answer. It was from Blix. She wrote:

"Don't you want to come up and play cards with me tonight? We haven't had a game in over a week?"

"How did she know?" thought Conde to himself—"how could she tell?" Aloud, he said:

"I can't join you fellows, after all. 'Despatch from the managing editor.' Some special detail or other."

For the first time since the previous evening Conde felt his spirits rise as he set off toward the Washington Street hill. But though he and Blix spent as merry an evening as they remembered in a long time, his nameless, formless irritation returned upon him almost as soon as he had bidden her good-night. It stayed with him all through the week, and told upon his work. As a result, three of his articles were thrown out by the editor.

"We can't run such rot as that in the paper," the chief had said. "Can't you give us a story?"

"Oh, I've got a kind of a yarn you can run if you like," answered Conde, his week's depression at its very lowest.

A Victory Over Death was published in the following Sunday's supplement of the *Times*, with illustrations by one of the staff artists. It attracted not the least attention.

Just before he went to bed the Sunday evening of its appearance, Conde read it over again for the last time.

"It's a rotten failure," he muttered gloomily as he cast the paper from him. "Simple drivel. I wonder what Blix will think of it. I wonder if I amount to a hill of beans. I wonder *what* she wants to go East for, anyway."

Chapter IX

The old-fashioned Union Street cable car, with its low, comfortable outside seats, put Blix and Conde down just inside the Presidio Government Reservation. Conde asked a direction of a sentry nursing his Krag-Jorgensen at the terminus of the track, and then with Blix set off down the long board walk through the tunnel of overhanging evergreens.

The day could not have been more desirable. It was a little after ten of a Monday morning, Condy's weekly holiday. The air was neither cool nor warm, effervescent merely, brisk and full of the smell of grass and of the sea. The sky was a speckless sheen of pale blue. To their right, and not far off, was the bay, blue as indigo. Alcatraz seemed close at hand; beyond was the enormous green, red, and purple pyramid of Tamalpais climbing out of the water, head and shoulders above the little foothills, and looking out to the sea and to the west.

The Reservation itself was delightful. There were rows of the officers' houses, all alike, drawn up in lines like an assembly of the staff; there were huge barracks, most like college dormitories; and on their porches enlisted men in shirt sleeves and overalls were cleaning saddles, and polishing the brass of head-stalls and bridles, whistling the while or smoking corn-cob pipes. Here on the parade-ground a soldier, his coat and vest removed, was batting grounders and flies to a half-dozen of his fellows. Over by the stables, strings of horses, all of the same color, were being curried and cleaned. A young lieutenant upon a bicycle spun silently past. An officer came from his front gate, his coat unbuttoned and a briar in his teeth. The walks and roads were flanked with lines of black-painted cannonballs; inverted pieces of abandoned ordnance stood at corners. From a distance came the mellow snarling of a bugle.

Blix and Conde had planned a long walk for that day. They were to go out through the Presidio Reservation, past the barracks and officers' quarters, and on to the old fort at the Golden Gate. Here they would turn and follow the shoreline for a way, then strike inland across the hills for a short half-mile, and regain the city and the streetcar lines by way of the golf-links. Conde had insisted upon wearing his bicycle outfit for the occasion, and, moreover, carried a little satchel, which, he said, contained a pair of shoes.

But Blix was as sweet as a rose that morning, all in tailor-made black but for the inevitable bands of white satin wrapped high and tight about her neck. The St. Bernard dog-collar did duty as a belt. She had disdained a veil, and her yellow hair was already blowing about her smooth pink cheeks. She walked at his side, her step as firm and solid as his own, her round, strong arms swinging, her little brown eyes shining with good spirits and vigor, and the pure, clean animal joy of being alive on that fine cool Western morning. She talked almost incessantly. She was positively garrulous. She talked about the fine day that it was, about the queer new forage caps of the soldiers, about the bare green hills of the Reservation, about the little cemetery they passed just beyond the limits of the barracks, about a rabbit she saw, and about the quail they both heard whistling and calling in the hollows under the bushes.

Conde walked at her side in silence, yet no less happy than she, smoking his pipe and casting occasional glances at a great ship—a four-master that was being towed out toward the Golden Gate. At every moment and at every turn they noted things that interested them, and to which they called each other's attention.

"Look, Blix!"

"Oh, Conde, look at that!"

They were soon out of the miniature city of the Post, and held on down through the low reach of tules and sand-dunes that stretch between the barracks and the old red fort.

"Look, Conde!" said Blix. "What's that building down there on the shore of the bay—the one with the flagstaff?"

"I think that must be the lifeboat station."

"I wonder if we could go down and visit it. I think it would be good fun."

"Idea!" exclaimed Conde.

The station was close at hand. To reach it they had but to leave the crazy board walk that led on toward the fort, and cross a few hundred yards of sand-dune. Conde opened the gate that broke the line of evergreen hedge around the little two-story house, and promptly unchained a veritable pandemonium of dogs.

Inside, the place was not without a certain charm of its own. A brick wall, bordered with shells, led to the front of the station, which gave directly upon the bay; a little well-kept lawn opened to right and left, and six or eight gaily-painted old rowboats were set about, half filled with loam in which fuchsias, geraniums, and mignonettes were flowering. A cat or two dozed upon the windowsills in the sun. Upon a sort of porch overhead, two of the crew paced up and down in a manner that at once suggested the poop. Here and there was a gleam of highly polished red copper or brass trimmings. The bay was within two steps of the front door, while a little further down the beach was the house where the surf-boat was kept, and the long runway leading down from it to the water. Conde rapped loudly at the front door. It was opened by Captain Jack.

Captain Jack, and no other; only now he wore a blue sweater and a leather-visored cap, with the letters U. S. L. B. S. around the band.

Not an instant was given them for preparation. The thing had happened with the abruptness of a transformation scene at a theater. Condy's knock had evoked a situation. Speech was stricken from their mouths. For a moment they were bereft even of action, and stood there on the threshold, staring open-mouthed and open-eyed at the sudden reappearance of their "matrimonial object." Conde was literally dumb; in the end it was Blix who tided them over the crisis.

"We were just going by—just taking a walk," she explained, "and we thought we'd like to see the station. Is it all right? Can we look around?"

"Why, of course," assented the Captain with great cordiality. "Come right in. This is visitors' day. You just happened to hit it—only it's mighty few visitors we ever have," he added.

While Conde was registering for himself and Blix, they managed to exchange a lightning glance. It was evident the Captain did not recognize them. The situation readjusted itself, even promised to be of extraordinary interest. And for that matter it made little difference whether the captain remembered them or not.

"No, we don't get many visitors," the Captain went on, as he led them out of the station and down the small gravel walk to the house where the surf-boat was kept. "This is a quiet station. People don't fetch out this way very often, and we're not called out very often, either. We're an inside post, you see, and usually we don't get a call unless the sea's so high that the Cliff House station can't launch their boat. So, you see, we don't go out much, but when we *do*, it means business with a great big B. Now, this here, you see," continued the Captain, rolling back the sliding doors of the house, "is the surf-boat. By the way, let's see; I ain't just caught your names yet."

"Well, my name's Rivers," said Conde, "and this is Miss Bessemer. We're both from the city."

"Happy to know you, sir; happy to know you, miss," he returned, pulling off his cap. "My name's Hoskins, but you can just call me Captain Jack. I'm so used to it that I don't kind of answer to the other. Well, now, Miss Bessemer, this here's the surf-boat; she's self-rightin', self-bailin', she can't capsize, and if I was to tell you how many thousands of dollars she cost, you wouldn't believe me."

Conde and Blix spent a delightful half-hour in the boat-house while Captain Jack explained and illustrated, and told them anecdotes of wrecks, escapes, and rescues till they held their breaths like ten-year-olds.

It did not take Conde long to know that he had discovered what the storyteller so often tells of but so seldom finds, and what, for want of a better name, he elects to call "a character."

Captain Jack had been everywhere, had seen everything, and had done most of the things worth doing, including a great many things that he had far better have left undone. But on this latter point the Captain seemed to be innocently and completely devoid of a moral sense of right and wrong. It was quite evident that he saw no matter for conscience in the smuggling of Chinamen across the, Canadian border at thirty dollars a head—a venture in which he had had the assistance of the prodigal son of an American divine of international renown. The trade to Peruvian insurgents of condemned rifles was to be regretted only because the ring manipulating it was broken up. The appropriation of a schooner in the harbor of Callao was a story in itself; while the robbery of thirty thousand dollars' worth of sea-otter skins from a Russian trading-post in Alaska, accomplished chiefly through the agency of a barrel of rum manufactured from sugarcane, was a veritable achievement.

He had been born, so he told them, in Winchester, in England, and—Heaven save the mark!—had been brought up with a view of taking orders. For some time he was a choir boy in the great Winchester Cathedral; then, while yet a lad, had gone to sea. He had been boat-steerer on a New Bedford whaler, and struck his first whale when only sixteen. He had filibustered down to Chili; had acted as ice pilot on an Arctic relief expedition; had captained a crew of Chinamen shark-fishing in Magdalena Bay, and had been nearly murdered by his men; had been a deep-sea diver, and had burst his eardrums at the business, so that now he could blow tobacco smoke out of his ears; he had been shipwrecked in the Gilberts, fought with the Seris on the lower California Islands, sold champagne—made from rock candy, effervescent salts, and Reisling wine—to the Coreans, had dreamed of "holding up" a Cunard liner, and had ridden on the Strand in a hansom with William Ewart Gladstone. But the one thing of which he was proud, the one picture of his life he most delighted to recall, was himself as manager of a negro minstrel troupe, in a hired drum-major's uniform, marching down the streets of Sacramento at the head of the brass band in burnt cork and regimentals.

"The star of the troupe," he told them, "was the lady with the iron jore. We busted in Stockton, and she gave me her diamonds to pawn. I pawned 'em, and kept back something in the hand for myself and hooked it to San Francisco. Strike me straight if she didn't follow me, that iron-jored piece; met me one day in front of the Bush Street Theater, and horse-whipped me properly. Now, just think of that"—and he laughed as though it was the best kind of a joke.

"But," hazarded Blix, "don't you find it rather dull out here—lonesome? I should think you would want to have someone with you to keep you company—to—to do your cooking for you?"

But Conde, ignoring her diplomacy and thinking only of possible stories, blundered off upon another track.

"Yes," he said, "you've led such a life of action, I should think this station would be pretty dull for you. How did you happen to choose it?"

"Well, you see," answered the Captain, leaning against the smooth white flank of the surf-boat, his hands in his pockets, "I'm lying low just now. I got into a scrape down at Libertad, in Mexico, that made talk, and I'm waiting for that to die down some. You see, it was this way."

Mindful of their experience with the mate of the whaleback, Conde and Blix were all attention in an instant. Blix sat down upon an upturned box, her elbows on her knees, leaning forward, her little eyes fixed and shining with interest and expectation; Conde, the storyteller all alive and vibrant in him, stood at her elbow, smoking cigarette after cigarette, his fingers dancing with excitement and animation as the Captain spoke.

And then it was that Conde and Blix, in that isolated station, the bay lapping at the shore within earshot, in that atmosphere redolent of paint and oakum and of seaweed decaying upon the beach outside, first heard the story of "In Defiance of Authority."

Captain Jack began it with his experience as a restaurant keeper during the boom days in Seattle, Washington. He told them how he was the cashier of a dining-saloon whose daily net profits exceeded eight hundred dollars; how its proprietor suddenly died, and how he, Captain Jack, continued the management of the restaurant pending a settlement of the proprietor's affairs and an appearance of heirs; how in the confusion and excitement of the boom no settlement was ever made; and how, no heirs appearing, he assumed charge of the establishment himself, paying bills, making contracts, and signing notes, until he came to consider the business and all its enormous profits as his own; and how at last, when the restaurant was burned, he found himself some forty thousand dollars "ahead of the game."

Then he told them of the strange club of the place, called "The Exiles," made up chiefly of "younger sons" of English and British-Canadian families, every member possessed of a "past" more or less disreputable; men who had left their country for their country's good, and for their family's peace of mind—adventurers, wanderers, soldiers of fortune, gentlemen-vagabonds, men of hyphenated names and even noble birth, whose appellations were avowedly aliases. He told them of his meeting with Billy Isham, one of the club's directors, and of the happy-go-lucky, reckless, unpractical character of the man; of their acquaintance, intimacy, and subsequent partnership; of how the filibustering project was started with Captain Jack's forty thousand, and the never-to-be-forgotten interview in San Francisco with Senora Estrada, the agent of the insurgents; of the incident of her calling-card—how she tore it in two and gave one-half to Isham; of their outfitting, and the broken sextant that was to cause their ultimate discomfiture and disaster, and of the voyage to the rendezvous on a Panama liner.

"Strike me!" continued Captain Jack, "you should have seen Billy Isham on that Panama dough-dish; a passenger ship she was, and Billy was the life of her from stem to stern-post. There was a church pulpit aboard that they were taking down to Mazatlan for some chapel or other, and this here pulpit was lashed on deck aft. Well, Billy had been most kinds of a fool in his life, and among others a play-actor; called himself Gaston Maundeville, and was clean daft on his knowledge of Shakespeare and his own power of interpretin' the hidden meanin' of the lines. I ain't never going to forget the day he gave us Portia's speech. We were just under the tropic, and the day was a scorcher. There was mostly men folk aboard, and we lay around the deck in our pajamas, while Billy—Gaston Maundeville, dressed in striped red and white pajamas—clum up in that bally pulpit, with the ship's Shakespeare in his hands, an' let us have—'The quality o' mercy isn't strained; it droppeth as the genteel dew from heavun.' Laugh, I tell you I was sore with it. Lord, how we guyed him! An' the more we guyed and the more we laughed, the more serious he got and the madder he grew. He said he was interpretin' the hidden meanin' of the lines."

And so the Captain ran through that wild, fiery tale—of fighting and loving, buccaneering and conspiring; mandolins tinkling, knives clicking; oaths mingling with sonnets, and spilled wine with spilled blood. He told them of Isham's knife duel with the Mexican lieutenant, their left wrists lashed together; of the "battle of the thirty" in the pitch dark of the Custom House cellar; of Senora Estrada's love for Isham; and all the roll and plunge of action that make up the story of "In Defiance of Authority."

At the end, Blix's little eyes were snapping like sparks; Condy's face was flaming, his hands were cold, and he was shifting his weight from foot to foot, like an excited thoroughbred horse.

"Heavens and earth, what a yarn!" he exclaimed almost in a whisper.

Blix drew a long, tremulous breath and sat back upon the upturned box, looking around her as though she had but that moment been awakened.

"Yes, sir," said the Captain, rolling a cigarette. "Yes, sir, those were great days. Get down there around the line in those little, out-o'-the-way republics along the South American coast, and things happen to you. You hold a man's life in the crook of your forefinger, an' nothing's done by halves. If you hate a man, you lay awake nights biting your mattress, just thinking how you hate him; an' if you love a woman—good Lord, how you do *love* her!"

"But—but!" exclaimed Conde, "I don't see how you can want to do anything else. Why, you're living sixty to the minute when you're playing a game like that!"

"Oh, I ain't dead yet!" answered the Captain. "I got a few schemes left that I could get fun out of."

"How can you wait a minute!" exclaimed Blix breathlessly. "Why don't you get a ship right away—tomorrow—and go right off on some other adventure?"

"Well, I can't just now," returned the Captain, blowing the smoke from his cigarette through his ears. "There's a good many reasons; one of 'em is that I've just been married."

Chapter X

"Mum—mar—married!" gasped Conde, swallowing something in his throat.

Blix rose to her feet.

"Just been *married*!" she repeated, a little frightened. "Why—why—why; how *delightful*!"

"Yes—yes," mumbled Conde. "How delightful. I congratulate you!"

"Come in—come back to the station," said the Captain jovially, "and I'll introduce you to m' wife. We were married only last Sunday."

"Why, yes—yes, of course, we'd be delighted," vociferated the two conspirators a little hysterically.

"She's a mighty fine little woman," declared the Captain, as he rolled the door of the boat-house to its place and preceded them up the gravel walk to the station.

"Of course she is," responded Blix. Behind Captain Jack's back she fixed Conde with a wide-eyed look, and nudged him fiercely with an elbow to recall him to himself; for Condy's wits were scattered like a flock of terrified birds, and he was gazing blankly at the Captain's coat collar with a vacant, maniacal smile.

"For Heaven's sake, Conde!" she had time to whisper before they arrived in the hallway of the station.

But fortunately they were allowed a minute or so to recover themselves and prepare for what was coming. Captain Jack ushered them into what was either the parlor, office, or sitting-room of the station, and left them with the words:

"Just make yourselves comfortable here, an' I'll go fetch the little woman."

No sooner had he gone than the two turned to each other.

"Well!"

"*Well!*"

"We're in for it now."

"But we must see it through, Conde; act just as natural as you can, and we're all right."

"But supposing *she* recognizes us!"

"Supposing she does—what then. How *are* they to know that we wrote the letters?"

"Sh, Blix, not so loud! They know by now that *they* didn't."

"But it seems that it hasn't made any difference to them; they are married. And besides, they wouldn't speak about putting 'personals' in the

89

paper to us. They would never let anybody know that."

"Do you suppose they could possibly suspect?"

"I'm sure they couldn't."

"Here they come."

"Keep perfectly calm, and we're saved."

"Suppose it isn't K. D. B., after all?"

But it was, of course, and she recognized them in an instant. She and the Captain—the latter all grins—came in from the direction of the kitchen, K. D. B. wearing a neat blue calico gown and an apron that was really a marvel of cleanliness and starch.

"Kitty!" exclaimed Captain Jack, seized again with an unexplainable mirth, "here's some young folks come out to see the place an' I want you to know 'em. Mr. Rivers, this is m' wife, Kitty, and—lessee, miss, I don't rightly remember your name."

"Bessemer!" exclaimed Conde and Blix in a breath.

"Oh!" exclaimed K. D. B., "you were in the restaurant the night that the Captain and I—I—that is—yes, I'm quite sure I've seen you before." She turned from one to the other. beginning to blush furiously.

"Yes, yes, in Luna's restaurant, wasn't it?" said Conde desperately. "It seems to me I do just barely remember."

"And wasn't the Captain there?" Blix ventured.

"I forgot my stick, I remember," continued Conde. "I came back for it; and just as I was going out it seems to me I saw you two at a table near the door."

He thought it best to allow their "matrimonial objects" to believe he had not seen them before.

"Yes, yes, we were there," answered K. D. B. tactfully. "We dine there almost every Monday night."

Blix guessed that K. D. B. would prefer to have the real facts of the situation ignored, and determined she should have the chance to change the conversation if she wished.

"What a delicious supper one has there!" she said.

"Can't say I like Mexican cooking myself," answered K. D. B., forgetting that they dined there every Monday night. "Plain United States is good enough for me."

Suddenly Captain Jack turned abruptly to Conde, exclaiming: "Oh, you was the chap that called the picture of that schooner a barkentine."

"Yes; *wasn't* that a barkentine?" he answered innocently.

"Barkentine your *eye!*" spluttered the Captain. "Why, that was a schooner as plain as a pie plate."

But ten minutes later the ordeal was over, and Blix and Conde, once more breathing easily, were on their walk again. The Captain and K. D. B. had even accompanied them to the gate of the station, and had strenuously urged them to "come in and see them again the next time they were out that way."

"Married!" murmured Conde, putting both hands to his head. "We've done it, we've done it now."

"Well, what of it?" declared Blix, a little defiantly. "I think it's all right. You can see the Captain is in love with her, and she with him. No, we've nothing to reproach ourselves with."

"But—but—but so sudden!" whispered Conde, all aghast. "That's what makes me faint—the suddenness of it."

"It shows how much they are in love, how—how readily they—adapted themselves to each other. No, it's all right."

"They seemed to like us—actually."

"Well, they had better—if they knew the truth. Without us they never would have met."

"They both asked us to come out and see them again, did you notice that? Let's do it, Blix," Conde suddenly exclaimed; "let's get to know them!"

"Of course we must. Wouldn't it be fun to call on them—to get regularly acquainted with them!"

"They might ask us to dinner some time."

"And think of the stories he could tell you!"

They enthused immediately upon this subject, both talking excitedly at the same time, going over the details of the Captain's yarns, recalling the incidents to each other.

"Fancy!" exclaimed Conde. "Fancy Billy Isham in his pajamas, red and white stripes, reading Shakespeare from that pulpit on board the ship, and the other men guying him! Isn't that a *scene* for you? Can't you just *see* it?"

"I wonder if the Captain wasn't making all those things up as he went along. He don't seem to have any sense of right and wrong at all. He might have been lying, Conde."

"What difference would that make?"

And so they went along in that fine, clear, Western morning, on the edge of the Continent, both of them young and strong and vigorous, the Pacific under their eyes, the great clean Trades blowing in their faces, the smell of the salt sea coming in long aromatic whiffs to their nostrils. Young and strong and fresh, their imaginations thronging with pictures of vigorous action and adventure, buccaneering, filibustering, and all the swing, the leap, the rush and gallop, the exuberant, strong life of the great, uncharted world of Romance.

And all unknowingly they were a Romance in themselves. Cynicism, old age, and the weariness of all things done had no place in the world in which they walked. They still had their illusions, all the keenness of their sensations, all the vividness of their impressions. The simple things of the world, the great, broad, primal emotions of the race stirred in them. As they swung along, going toward the ocean, their brains were almost as empty of thought or of reflection as those of two fine, clean animals. They were all for the immediate sensation; they did not think—they *felt*. The intellect was dormant; they looked at things, they heard things, they smelled the smell of the sea, and of the seaweed, of the fat, rank growth of cresses in the salt marshes; they turned their cheeks to the passing wind, and filled their mouths and breasts with it. Their life was sweet to them; every hour was one glad effervescence. The fact that the ocean was blue was a matter for rejoicing. It was good to be alive on that royal morning. Just to be young was an exhilaration; and everything was young with them—the day was young, the country was young, and the civilization to which they belonged, teeming there upon the green, Western fringe of the continent, was young and heady and tumultuous with the boisterous, red blood of a new race.

Conde even forgot, or rather disdained on such a morning as that, to piece together and rearrange Captain Jack's yarns into story form. To look at the sea and the green hills, to watch the pink on Blix's cheek and her yellow hair blowing across her eyes and lips, was better than thinking. Life was better than literature. To live was better than to read; one live human being was better than ten thousand Shakespeares; an act was better than a thought. Why, just to love Blix, to be with her, to see the sweet, clean flush of her cheek, to know that she was there at his side, and to have the touch of her elbow as they walked, was better than the best story, the greatest novel he could ever hope to write. Life was better than literature, and love was the best thing in life. To love Blix and to be near her—what else was worth while? Could he ever think of finding anything in life sweeter and finer than this dear young girl of nineteen?

Suddenly Conde came to himself with an abrupt start. What was this he was thinking—what was this he was telling himself? Love Blix! He loved

Blix! Why, of *course* he loved her—loved her so, that with the thought of it there came a great, sudden clutch at the heart and a strange sense of tenderness, so vague and yet so great that it eluded speech and all expression. Love her! Of course he loved her! He had, all unknowing, loved her even before this wonderful morning: had loved her that day at the lake, and that never-to-be-forgotten, delicious afternoon in the Chinese restaurant; all those long, quiet evenings spent in the window of the little dining-room, looking down upon the darkening city, he had loved her. Why, all his days for the last few months had been full of the love of her.

How else had he been so happy? how else did it come about that little by little he was withdrawing from the society and influence of his artificial world, as represented by such men as Sargeant? how else was he slowly loosening the grip of the one evil and vicious habit that had clutched him so long? how else was his ambition stirring? how else was his hitherto aimless enthusiasm hardening to energy and determination? She had not always so influenced him. In the days when they had just known each other, and met each other in the weekly course of their formal life, it had not been so, even though they pretended a certain amount of affection. He remembered the evening when Blix had brought those days to an abrupt end, and how at the moment he had told himself that after all he had never known the real Blix. Since then, in the charming, unconventional life they had led, everything had been changed. He had come to know her for what she was, to know her genuine goodness, her sincerity, her contempt of affectations, her comradeship, her calm, fine strength and unbroken good nature; and day by day, here a little and there a little, his love for her had grown so quietly, so evenly, that he had never known it, until now, behold! It was suddenly come to flower, full and strong—a flower whose fragrance had suddenly filled all his life and all his world with its sweetness.

Half an hour after leaving the lifeboat station, Conde and Blix reached the old, red-brick fort, deserted, abandoned, and rime-incrusted, at the entrance of the Golden Gate. They turned its angle, and there rolled the Pacific, a blue floor of shifting water, stretching out there forever and forever over the curve of the earth, over the shoulder of the world, with never a sail in view and never a break from horizon to horizon.

They followed down the shore, sometimes upon the old and broken flume that runs along the seaward face of the hills that rise from the beach, or sometimes upon the beach itself, stepping from boulder to boulder, or holding along at the edge of the water upon reaches of white, hard sand.

The beach was solitary; not a soul was in sight. Close at hand, to landward, great hills, bare and green, shut off the sky; and here and there the land came tumbling down into the sea in great, jagged, craggy rocks, knee-deep in swirling foam, and all black with wet. The air was full of the prolonged thunder of the surf, and at intervals sea-birds passed overhead with an occasional piping cry. Wreckage was tumbled about here and there; and innumerable cocoanut shards, huge, brown cups of fuzzy bark, lay underfoot and in the crevices of the rocks. They found a jelly-fish—a pulpy translucent mass; and once even caught a sight of a seal in the hollow of a breaker, with sleek and shining head, his barbels bristling, and heard his hoarse croaking bark as he hunted the off-shore fish.

Blix refused to allow Conde to help her in the least. She was quite as active and strong as he, and clambered from rock to rock and over the shattered scantling of the flume with the vigor and agility of a young boy. She muddied her shoes to the very tops scratched her hands, tore her skirt, and even twisted her ankle; but her little eyes were never so bright, nor was the pink flush of her cheeks ever more adorable. And she was never done talking—a veritable chatterbox. She saw everything and talked about everything she saw, quite indifferent as to whether or no Conde listened. Now it was a queer bit of seaweed, now it was a group of gulls clamoring over a dead fish, now a purple starfish, now a breaker of unusual size. Her splendid vitality carried her away. She was excited, alive to her very fingertips, vibrant to the least sensation, quivering to the least impression.

"Let's get up here and sit down somewhere," said Conde, at length.

They left the beach and climbed up the slope of the hills, near a point where a long arm of land thrust out into the sea and shut off the wind; a path was there, and they followed it for a few yards, till they had come to a little amphitheater surrounded with blackberry bushes.

Here they sat down, Blix settling herself on an old log with a little sigh of contentment, Conde stretching himself out, a new-lighted pipe in his teeth, his head resting on the little handbag he had persistently carried ever since morning. Then Blix fell suddenly silent, and for a long time the two sat there without speaking, absorbed in the enjoyment of looking at the enormous green hills rolling down to the sea, the breakers thundering at the beach, the gashed pinnacles of rock, the vast reach of the Pacific, and the distant prospect of the old fort at the entrance of the Golden Gate.

"We might be a thousand miles away from the city, for all the looks of it, mightn't we, Conde?" said Blix, after a while. "And I'm that *hungry*! It must be nearly noon."

For answer, Conde sat up with profound gravity, and with a great air of nonchalance opened the handbag, and, instead of shoes took out, first, a pint bottle of claret, then "devilish" ham sandwiches in oiled paper, a bottle of stuffed olives, a great bag of salted almonds, two little tumblers, a paper-covered novel, and a mouth organ.

Blix fairly crowed with delight, clasping her hands upon her knees, and rocking to and fro where she sat upon the log.

"Oh, Conde, and you thought of a *lunch*—you said it was shoes—and you remembered I loved stuffed olives, too; and a book to read. What is it—*The Seven Seas*. No, I never *was* so happy. But the mouth organ—what's that for?"

"To play on. What did you think—think it was a can-opener?"

Blix choked with merriment over his foolery, and Conde added proudly:

"Look there! I made those sandwiches!"

They looked as though he had—great, fat chunks of bread, the crust still on; the "devilish" ham in thick strata between; and, positively, he had *buttered* the bread. But it was all one with them; they ate as though at a banquet, and Blix even took off her hat and hung it upon one of the nearby bushes. Of course Conde had forgotten a corkscrew. He tried to dig out the cork of the claret bottle with his knife, until he had broken both blades and was about to give up in despair, when Blix, at the end of her patience, took the bottle from him and pushed in the cork with her finger.

"Wine, music, literature, and feasting," observed Conde. "We're getting regularly luxurious, just like Sardine-apalus."

But Conde himself had suddenly entered into an atmosphere of happiness, the like of which he had never known or dreamed of before. He loved Blix—he had just discovered it. He loved her because she was so genuine, so radiantly fresh and strong; loved her because she liked the things that he liked, because they two looked at the world from precisely the same point of view, hating shams and affectations, happy in the things that were simple and honest and natural. He loved her because she liked his books, appreciating the things therein that he appreciated, liking what he liked, disapproving of what he condemned. He loved her because she was nineteen, and because she was so young and unspoiled and was happy just because the ocean was blue and the morning fine. He loved her because she was so pretty, because of the softness of her yellow hair, because of her round, white forehead and pink cheeks, because of her little, dark-brown eyes, with that look in them as if she were just done smiling or just about to smile, one could not say which; loved her because of her good, firm mouth and chin, because of her full neck and its high, tight bands of white satin. And he loved her because her arms were strong and round, and because she wore the great dog-collar around her trim, firm-corseted waist, and because there emanated from her with every movement a barely perceptible, delicious, feminine odor, that was in part perfume, but mostly a subtle, vague aroma, charming beyond words, that came from her mouth, her hair, her neck, her arms, her whole sweet personality. And he loved her because she was herself, because she was Blix, because of that strange, sweet influence that was disengaged from her in those quiet moments when she seemed so close to him, when some unnamed, mysterious sixth sense in him stirred and woke and told him of her goodness, of her clean purity and womanliness; and that certain, vague tenderness in him went out toward her, a tenderness not for her only, but for all the good things of the world; and he felt his nobler side rousing up and the awakening of the desire to be his better self.

Covertly he looked at her, as she sat near him, her yellow hair rolling and blowing back from her forehead, her hands clasped over her knee, looking out over the ocean, thoughtful, her eyes wide.

She had told him she did not love him. Conde remembered that perfectly well. She was sincere in the matter; she did not love him. That subject had been once and for all banished from their intercourse. And it was because of that very reason that their companionship of the last three or four months had been so charming. She looked upon him merely as a chum. She had not changed in the least from that time until now, whereas he—why, all his world was new for him that morning! Why, he loved her so, she had become so dear to him, that the very thought of her made his heart swell and leap.

But he must keep all this to himself. If he spoke to her, told her of how he loved her, it would spoil and end their companionship upon the instant. They had both agreed upon that; they had tried the other, and it had worked out. As lovers they had wearied of each other; as chums they had been perfectly congenial, thoroughly and completely happy.

Conde set his teeth. It was a hard situation. He must choose between bringing an end to this charming comradeship of theirs, or else fight back all show of love for her, keep it down and under hand, and that at a time when every nerve of him quivered like a smitten harp-string. It was not in him or in his temperament to love her calmly, quietly, or at a distance; he wanted the touch of her hand, the touch of her cool, smooth cheek, the delicious aroma of her breath in his nostrils her lips against his, her hair and all its fragrance in his face.

"Conde, what's the matter?" Blix was looking at him with an expression of no little concern. "What are you frowning so about, and clinching your fists? And you're pale, too. What's gone wrong?"

He shot a glance at her, and bestirred himself sharply.

"Isn't this a jolly little corner?" he said. "Blix, how long is it before you go?"

"Six weeks from tomorrow."

"And you're going to be gone four years—four years! Maybe you never will come back. Can't tell what will happen in four years. Where's the blooming mouth-organ?"

But the mouth-organ was full of crumbs. Conde could not play on it. To all his efforts it responded only by gasps, mournfulest death-rattles, and lamentable wails. Conde hurled it into the sea.

"Well, where's the blooming book, then?" he demanded. "You're sitting on it, Blix. Here, read something in it. Open it anywhere."

"No; you read to me."

"I will not. Haven't I done enough? Didn't I buy the book and get the lunch, and make the sandwiches, and pay the car-fare? I think this expedition will cost me pretty near three dollars before we're through with the day. No; the least you can do is to read to me. Here, we'll match for it."

Conde drew a dime from his pocket, and Blix a quarter from her purse.

"You're matching me," she said.

Conde tossed the coin and lost, and Blix said, as he picked up the book:

"For a man that has such unvarying bad luck as you, gambling is just simple madness. You and I have never played a game of poker yet that I've not won every cent of money you had."

"Yes; and what are you doing with it all?"

"Spending it," she returned loftily; "gloves and veils and lace pins—all kinds of things."

But Conde knew the way she spoke that this was not true.

For the next hour or so he read to her from "The Seven Seas," while the afternoon passed, the wind stirring the chaparral and blackberry bushes in the hollows of the huge, bare hills, the surf rolling and grumbling on the beach below, the sea-birds wheeling overhead. Blix listened intently, but Conde could not have told of what he was reading. Living was better than reading, life was better than literature, and his new-found love for her was poetry enough for him. He read so that he might not talk to her or look at her, for it seemed to him at times as though some second self in him would speak and betray him in spite of his best efforts. Never before in all his life had he been so happy; never before had he been so troubled. He began to jumble the lines and words as he read, over-running periods, even turning two pages at once.

"What a splendid line!" Blix exclaimed.

"What line—what—what are you talking about? Blix, let's always remember today. Let's make a promise, no matter what happens or where we are, let's always write to each other on the anniversary of today. What do you say?"

"Yes; I'll promise—and you—"

"I'll promise faithfully. Oh, I'll never forget today nor—yes, yes, I'll promise—why, today—Blix—where's that damn book gone?"

"Conde!"

"Well, I can't find the book. You're sitting on it again. Confound the book, anyway! Let's walk some more."

"We've a long ways to go if we're to get home in time for supper. Let's go to Luna's for supper."

"I never saw such a girl as you to think of ways for spending money. What kind of a purse-proud plutocrat do you think I am? I've only seventy-five cents left. How much have you got?"

Blix had fifty-five cents in her purse, and they had a grave council over their finances. They had just enough for car-fare and two "suppers Mexican," with ten cents left over.

"That's for Richard's tip," said Blix.

"That's for my *cigar*," he retorted.

"You made ME give him fifty cents. You said it was the least I could offer him—noblesse oblige."

"Well, then, I *couldn't* offer him a dime, don't you see? I'll tell him we are broke this time."

They started home, not as they had come, but climbing the hill and going across a breezy open down, radiant with blue iris, wild heliotrope, yellow poppies, and even a violet here and there. A little further on they gained one of the roads of the Reservation, red earth smooth as a billiard table; and just at an angle where the road made a sharp elbow and trended cityward, they paused for a moment and looked down and back at the superb view of the ocean, the vast half-moon of land, and the rolling hills in the foreground tumbling down toward the beach and all spangled with wild flowers.

Some fifteen minutes later they reached the golf-links.

"We can go across the links," said Conde, "and strike any number of car lines on the other side."

They left the road and struck across the links, Conde smoking his new-lighted pipe. But as they came around the edge of a long line of eucalyptus trees near the teeing ground, a warning voice suddenly called out:

"Fore!"

Conde and Blix looked up sharply, and there in a group not twenty feet away, in tweeds and "knickers," in smart, short golfing skirts and plaid cloaks, they saw young Sargeant and his sister, two other girls whom they knew as members of the fashionable "set," and Jack Carter in the act of swinging his driving iron.

Chapter XI

As the clock in the library of the club struck midnight, Conde laid down his pen, shoved the closely written sheets of paper from him, and leaned back in his chair, his fingers to his tired eyes. He was sitting at a desk in one of the further corners of the room and shut off by a great Japanese screen. He was in his shirt-sleeves, his hair was tumbled, his fingers ink-stained, and his face a little pale.

Since late in the evening he had been steadily writing. Three chapters of "In Defiance of Authority" were done, and he was now at work on the fourth. The day after the excursion to the Presidio—that wonderful event which seemed to Conde to mark the birthday of some new man within him—the idea had suddenly occurred to him that Captain Jack's story of the club of the exiles, the boom restaurant, and the filibustering expedition was precisely the novel of adventure of which the Centennial Company had spoken. At once he had set to work upon it, with an enthusiasm that, with shut teeth, he declared would not be lacking in energy. The story would have to be written out of his business hours. That meant he would have to give up his evenings to it. But he had done this, and for nearly a week had settled himself to his task in the quiet corner of the club at eight o'clock, and held to it resolutely until twelve.

The first two chapters had run off his pen with delightful ease. The third came harder; the events and incidents of the story became confused and contradictory; the character of Billy Isham obstinately refused to take the prominent place which Conde had designed for him; and with the beginning of the fourth chapter, Conde had finally come to know the enormous difficulties, the exasperating complications, the discouragements that begin anew with every paragraph, the obstacles that refuse to be surmounted, and all the pain, the labor, the downright mental travail and anguish that fall to the lot of the writer of novels.

To write a short story with the end in plain sight from the beginning was an easy matter compared to the upbuilding, grain by grain, atom by atom, of the fabric of "In Defiance of Authority." Conde soon found that there was but one way to go about the business. He must shut his eyes to the end of his novel—that far-off, divine event—and take his task chapter by chapter, even paragraph by paragraph; grinding out the tale, as it were, by main strength, driving his pen from line to line, hating the effort, happy only with the termination of each chapter, and working away, hour by hour, minute by minute, with the dogged, sullen, hammer-and-tongs obstinacy of the galley-slave, scourged to his daily toil.

At times the tale, apparently out of sheer perversity, would come to a full stop. To write another word seemed beyond the power of human ingenuity, and for an hour or more Conde would sit scowling at the half-written page, gnawing his nails, scouring his hair, dipping his pen into the ink-well, and squaring himself to the sheet of paper, all to no purpose.

There was no pleasure in it for him. A character once fixed in his mind, a scene once pictured in his imagination, and even before he had written a word the character lost the charm of its novelty, the scene the freshness of its original conception. Then, with infinite painstaking and with a patience little short of miraculous, he must slowly build up, brick by brick, the plan his brain had outlined in a single instant. It was all work—hard, disagreeable, laborious work; and no juggling with phrases, no false notions as to the "delight of creation," could make it appear otherwise. "And for what," he muttered as he rose, rolled up his sheaf of manuscript, and put on his coat; "what do I do it for, I don't know."

It was beyond question that, had he begun his novel three months before this time, Conde would have long since abandoned the hateful task. But Blix had changed all that. A sudden male force had begun to develop in Conde. A master-emotion had shaken him, and he had commenced to see and to feel the serious, more abiding, and perhaps the sterner side of life. Blix had steadied him, there was no denying that. He was not quite the same boyish, hare-brained fellow who had made "a buffoon of himself" in the Chinese restaurant, three months before.

The cars had stopped running by the time Conde reached the street. He walked home and flung himself to bed, his mind tired, his nerves unstrung, and all the blood of his body apparently concentrated in his brain. Working at night after writing all day long was telling upon him, and he knew it.

What with his work and his companionship with Blix, Conde soon began to drop out of his wonted place in his "set." He was obliged to decline one invitation after another that would take him out in the evening, and instead of lunching at his club with Sargeant or George Hands, as he had been accustomed to do at one time, he fell into another habit of lunching with Blix at the flat on Washington Street, and spending the two hours allowed to him in the middle of the day in her company.

Condy's desertion of them was often spoken of by the men of his club with whom he had been at one time so intimate, and the subject happened to be brought up again one noon when Jack Carter was in the club as

George Hands' guest. Hands, Carter, and Eckert were at one of the windows over their after-dinner cigars and liqueurs.

"I say," said Eckert suddenly, "who's that girl across the street there—the one in black, just going by that furrier's sign? I've seen her somewhere before. Know who it is?"

"That's Miss Bessemer, isn't it?" said George Hands, leaning forward. "Rather a stunning-looking girl."

"Yes, that's Travis Bessemer," assented Jack Carter; adding, a moment later, "it's too bad about that girl."

"What's the matter?" asked Eckert.

Carter lifted a shoulder. "Isn't *anything* the matter as far as I know, only somehow the best people have dropped her. She *used* to be received everywhere."

"Come to think, I *haven't* seen her out much this season," said Eckert. "But I heard she had bolted from 'Society' with the big S, and was going East—going to study medicine, I believe."

"I've always noticed," said Carter, with a smile, "that so soon as a girl is declassee, she develops a purpose in life and gets earnest, and all that sort of thing.

"Oh, well, come," growled George Hands, "Travis Bessemer is not declassee."

"I didn't say she was," answered Carter; "but she has made herself talked about a good deal lately. Going around with Rivers, as she does, isn't the most discreet thing in the world. Of course, it's all right, but it all makes talk, and I came across them by a grove of trees out on the links the other day—"

"Yes," observed Sargeant, leaning on the back of Carter's armchair; "yes; and I noticed, too, that she cut you dead. You fellows should have been there," he went on, in perfect good humor, turning to the others. "You missed a good little scene. Rivers and Miss Bessemer had been taking a tramp over the Reservation—and, by the way, it's a great place to walk, so my sister tells me; she and Dick Forsythe take a constitutional out there every Saturday morning—well, as I was saying, Rivers and Miss Bessemer came upon our party rather unexpectedly. We were all togged out in our golfing bags, and I presume we looked more like tailor's models, posing for the gallery, than people who were taking an outing; but Rivers and Miss Bessemer had been regularly exercising; looked as though they had done their fifteen miles since morning. They had their old clothes on, and they were dusty and muddy.

"You would have thought that a young girl such as Miss Bessemer is— for she's very young—would have been a little embarrassed at running up against such a spick-and-span lot as we were. Not a bit of it; didn't lose her poise for a moment. She bowed to my sister and to me, as though from the top of a drag, by Jove! And as though she were fresh from Redfern and Virot. You know a girl that can manage herself that way is a thoroughbred. She even remembered to cut little Johnnie Carter here, because Johnnie forced himself upon her one night at a dance when he was drunk; didn't she, Johnnie? Johnnie came up to her there, out on the links, fresh as a daisy, and put out his hand, with, 'Why, how do you do, Miss Bessemer?' and 'wherever did you come from?' and 'I haven't seen you in so long'; and she says, 'No, not since our last dance, I believe, Mr. Carter,' and looked at his hand as though it was something funny. Little Johnnie mumbled and flushed and stammered and backed off; and it was well that he did, because Rivers had begun to get red around the wattles. I say the little girl is a thoroughbred, and my sister wants to give her a dinner as soon as she comes out. But Johnnie says she's declassée, so may be my sister had better think it over."

"I didn't say she was declassée," exclaimed Carter. "I only said she would do well to be more careful."

Sargeant shifted his cigar to the other corner of his mouth, one eye shut to avoid the smoke.

"One might say as much of lots of people," he answered.

"I don't like your tone!" Carter flared out.

"Oh, go to the devil, Johnnie! Shall we all have a drink?"

On the Friday evening of that week, Conde set himself to his work at his accustomed hour. But he had had a hard day on the *Times*, Supplement, and his brain, like an overdriven horse, refused to work. In half an hour he had not written a paragraph.

"I thought it would be better, in the end, to loaf for one evening," he explained to Blix, some twenty minutes later, as they settled themselves in the little dining-room. "I can go at it better tomorrow. See how you like this last chapter."

Blix was enthusiastic over *In Defiance of Authority*. Conde had told her the outline of the story, and had read to her each chapter as he finished it.

"It's the best thing you have ever done, Conde, and you know it. I suppose it has faults, but I don't care anything about them. It's the story itself that's so interesting. After that first chapter of the boom restaurant and the exiles' club, nobody would want to lay the book down. You're doing the best work of your life so far, and you stick to it."

"It's grinding out copy for the Supplement at the same time that takes all the starch out of me. You've no idea what it means to write all day, and then sit down and write all evening."

"I *wish* you could get off the *Times*," said Blix. "You're just giving the best part of your life to hack work, and *now* it's interfering with your novel. I know you could do better work on your novel if you didn't have to work on the *Times*, couldn't you?"

"Oh, if you come to that, of course I could," he answered. "But they won't give me a vacation. I was sounding the editor on it day before yesterday. No; I'll have to manage somehow to swing the two together."

"Well, let's not talk shop now. Conde. You need a rest. Do you want to play poker?"

They played for upward of an hour that evening, and Conde, as usual, lost. His ill-luck was positively astonishing. During the last two months he had played poker with Blix on an average of three or four evenings in the week. and at the close of every game it was Blix who had all the chips.

Blix had come to know the game quite as well, if not better, than he. She could almost invariably tell when Conde held a good hand, but on her part could assume an air of indifference absolutely inscrutable.

"Cards?" said Conde, picking up the deck after the deal.

"I'll stand pat, Conde."

"The deuce you say," he answered, with a stare. "I'll take three."

"I'll pass it up to you," continued Blix gravely.

"Well—well, I'll bet you five chips."

"Raise you twenty."

Conde studied his hand, laid down the cards, picked them up again, scratched his head, and moved uneasily in his place. Then he threw down two high pairs.

"No," he said; "I won't see you. What did you have? Let's see, just for the fun of it."

Blix spread her cards on the table.

"Not a blessed thing!" exclaimed Conde. "I might have known it. There's my last dollar gone, too. Lend me fifty cents, Blix."

Blix shook her head.

"Why, what a little niggard!" he exclaimed aggrievedly. "I'll pay them all back to you."

"Now, why should I lend you money to play against me? I'll not give you a chip; and, besides, I don't want to play any more. Let's stop."

"I've a mind to stop for good; stop playing even with you."

Blix gave a little cry of joy.

"Oh, Conde, will you, could you? and never, never touch a card again? never play for money? I'd be so happy—but don't unless you know you would keep your promise. I would much rather have you play every night, down there at your club, than break your promise."

Conde fell silent, biting thoughtfully at the knuckle of a forefinger.

"Think twice about it, Conde," urged Blix; "because this would be for always."

Conde hesitated; then, abstractedly and as though speaking to himself:

"It's different now. Before we took that—three months ago, I don't say. It was harder for me to quit then, but now—well, everything is different now; and it would please you, Blixy!"

"More than anything else I can think of, Conde."

He gave her his hand.

"That settles it," he said quietly. "I'll never gamble again, Blix."

Blix gripped his hand hard, then jumped up, and, with a quick breath of satisfaction, gathered up the cards and chips and flung them into the fireplace.

"Oh, I'm so glad that's over with," she exclaimed, her little eyes dancing. "I've pretended to like it, but I've hated it all the time. You don't know *how* I've hated it! What men can see in it to make them sit up all night long is beyond me. And you truly mean, Conde, that you never will gamble again? Yes, I know you mean it this time. Oh, I'm so happy I could sing!"

"Good Heavens, don't do that!" he cried quickly. "You're a nice, amiable girl, Blix, even if you're not pretty, and you—"

"Oh, bother you!" she retorted; "but you promise?"

"On my honor."

"That's enough," she said quietly.

But even when "loafing" as he was this evening, Conde could not rid himself of the thought and recollection of his novel; resting or writing, it haunted him. Otherwise he would not have been the story-writer that he was. From now on until he should set down the last sentence, the "thing" was never to let him alone, never to allow him a moment's peace. He could think of nothing else, could talk of nothing else; every faculty of his brain, every sense of observation or imagination incessantly concentrated themselves upon this one point.

As they sat in the bay window watching the moon rise, his mind was still busy with it, and he suddenly broke out:

"I ought to work some kind of a *treasure* into the yarn. What's a story of adventure without a treasure? By Jove, Blix, I wish I could give my whole time to this stuff! It's ripping good material, and it ought to be handled as carefully as glass. Ought to be worked up, you know."

"Conde," said Blix, looking at him intently, "what is it stands in your way of leaving the *Times*? Would they take you back if you left them long enough to write your novel? You could write it in a month, couldn't you, if you had nothing else to do? Suppose you left them for a month—would they hold your place for you?"

"Yes—yes, I think they would; but in the meanwhile, Blix—there's the rub. I've never saved a cent out of my salary. When I stop, my pay stops, and wherewithal would I be fed? What are you looking for in that drawer—matches? Here, I've got a match."

Blix faced about at the sideboard, shutting the drawer by leaning against it. In both hands she held one of the delft sugar-bowls. She came up to the table, and emptied its contents upon the blue denim table-cover—two or three gold pieces, some fifteen silver dollars, and a handful of small change.

Disregarding all Condy's inquiries, she counted it, making little piles of the gold and silver and nickel pieces.

"Thirty-five and seven is forty-two," she murmured, counting off on her fingers, "and six is forty-eight, and ten is fifty-eight, and ten is sixty-eight; and here is ten, twenty, thirty, fifty-five cents in change." She thrust it all toward him, across the table. "There," she said, "is your wherewithal."

Conde stared. "My wherewithal!" he muttered.

"It ought to be enough for over a month."

"Where did you get all that? Whose is it?"

"It's your money, Conde. You loaned it to me, and now it has come in very handy."

"I *loaned* it to you?"

"It's the money I won from you during the time you've been playing poker with me. You didn't know it would amount to so much, did you?"

"Pshaw, I'll not touch it!" he exclaimed, drawing back from the money as though it was red-hot.

"Yes, you will," she told him. "I've been saving it up for you, Conde, every penny of it, from the first day we played down there at the lake; and I always told myself that the moment you made up your mind to quit playing, I would give it back to you."

"Why, the very idea!" he vociferated, his hands deep in his pockets, his face scarlet. "It's—it's preposterous, Blix! I won't let you *talk* about it even—I won't touch a nickel of that money. But, Blix, you're—you're—the finest woman I ever knew. You're a man's woman, that's what you are." He set his teeth. "If you loved a man, you'd be a regular pal to him; you'd back him up, you'd stand by him till the last gun was fired. I could do *anything* if a *woman* like you cared for me. Why, Blix, I—you haven't any idea—" He cleared his throat, stopping abruptly.

"But you must take this money," she answered; "*your* money. If you didn't, Conde, it would make me out nothing more nor less than a gambler. I wouldn't have dreamed of playing cards with you if I had ever intended to keep one penny of your money. From the very start I intended to keep it for you, and give it back to you so soon as you would stop; and now you have a chance to put this money to a good use. You don't have to stay on the *Times* now. You can't do your novel justice while you are doing your hack work at the same time, and I do so want *In Defiance of Authority* to be a success. I've faith in you, Conde. I know if you got the opportunity you would make a success."

"But you and I have played like two men playing," exclaimed Conde. "How would it look if Sargeant, say, should give me back the money he had won from me? What a cad I would be to take it!"

"That's just it—we've not played like two men. Then I *would* have been a gambler. I've played with you because I thought it would make a way for you to break off with the habit; and knowing as I did how fond you were of playing cards and how bad it was for you, how wicked it would have been for me to have played with you in any other spirit! Don't you see? And as it has turned out, you've given up playing, and you've enough money to make it possible for you to write your novel. The Centennial Company have asked you to try a story of adventure for them, you've found one that is splendid, you're just the man who could handle it, and now you've got the money to make it possible. Conde," she exclaimed suddenly, "don't you see your *chance*? Aren't you a big enough man to see your chance when it comes? And, besides, do you think I would take *money* from you? Can't you understand? If you don't take this money that belongs to you, you would insult me. That is just the way I would feel about it. You must see that. If you care for me at all, you'll take it."

*   *   *

The editor of the Sunday Supplement put his toothpick behind his ear and fixed Conde with his eyeglasses.

"Well, it's like this, Rivers," he said. "Of course, you know your own business best. If you stay on here with us, it will be all right. But I may as well tell you that I don't believe I can hold your place for a month. I can't get a man in here to do your work for just a month, and then fire him out at the end of that time. I don't like to lose you, but if you have an opportunity to get in on another paper during this vacation of yours, you're at liberty to do so, for all of me."

"Then you think my chance of coming back here would be pretty slim if I leave for a month now?"

"That's right."

There was a silence. Conde hesitated; then he rose.

"I'll take the chance," he announced.

To Blix, that evening, as he told her of the affair, he said: "It's neck or nothing now, Blix."

Chapter XII

BUT did Blix care for him?

In the retired corner of his club, shut off by the Japanese screen, or going up and down the city to and from his work, or sitting with her in the bay window of the little dining-room looking down upon the city, blurred in the twilight or radiant with the sunset, Conde asked himself the question. A score of times each day he came to a final, definite, negative decision; and a score of times reopened the whole subject. Beyond the fact that Blix had enjoyed herself in his company during the last months, Conde could find no sign or trace of encouragement; and for that matter he told himself that the indications pointed rather in the other direction. She had no compunction in leaving him to go away to New York, perhaps never to return. In less than a month now all their companionship was to end, and he would probably see the last of her.

He dared not let her know that at last he had really come to love her—that it was no pretense now; for he knew that with such declaration their "good times" would end even before she should go away. But every day; every hour that they were together made it harder for him to keep himself within bounds.

What with this trouble on his mind and the grim determination with which he held to his work, Conde changed rapidly. Blix had steadied him, and a certain earnestness and seriousness of purpose, a certain *strength* he had not known before, came swiftly into being.

Was Blix to go away, leave him, perhaps for all time, and not know how much he cared? Would he speak before she went? Conde did not know. It was a question that circumstances would help him to decide. He would not speak, so he resolved, unless he was sure that she cared herself; and if she did, she herself would give him a cue, a hint whereon to speak. But days went by, the time set for Blix's departure drew nearer and nearer, and yet she gave him not the slightest sign.

These two interests had now absorbed his entire life for the moment—his love for Blix, and his novel. Little by little "In Defiance of Authority" took shape. The boom restaurant and the club of the exiles were disposed of, Billy Isham began to come to the front, the filibustering expedition and Senora Estrada (with her torn calling card) had been introduced, and the expedition was ready to put to sea. But here a new difficulty was encountered.

"What do I know about ships?" Conde confessed to Blix. "If Billy

Isham is going to command a filibustering schooner, I've got to know something about a schooner—appear to, anyhow. I've got to know nautical lingo, the real thing, you know. I don't believe a *real* sailor ever in his life said 'belay there,' or 'avast.' We'll have to go out and see Captain Jack; get some more technical detail."

This move was productive of the most delightful results. Captain Jack was all on fire with interest the moment that Conde and Blix told him of the idea.

"An' you're going to put Billy Isham in a book. Well, strike me straight, that's a snorkin' good idea. I've always said that all Billy needed was a ticket seller an' an advance agent, an' he was a whole show in himself."

"We're going to send it East," said Blix, "as soon as it's finished, and have it published."

"Well, it ought to make prime readin', Miss; an' that's a good fetchin' title, *In Defiance of Authority.*"

Regularly Wednesday and Sunday afternoons, Blix and Conde came out to the lifeboat station. Captain Jack received them in sweater and visored cap, and ushered them into the front room.

"Well, how's the yarn getting on?" Captain Jack would ask.

Then Conde would read the last chapter while the Captain paced the floor, frowning heavily, smoking cigars, listening to every word. Conde told the story in the first person, as if Billy Isham's partner were narrating scenes and events in which he himself had moved. Conde called this protagonist "Burke Cassowan," and was rather proud of the name. But the captain would none of it. Cassowan, the protagonist, was simply "Our Mug."

"Now," Conde would say, notebook in hand, "now, Cap., we've got down to Mazatlan. Now I want to sort of organize the expedition in this next chapter."

"I see, I see," Captain Jack would exclaim, interested at once. "Wait a bit till I take off my shoes. I can think better with my shoes off"; and having removed his shoes, he would begin to pace the room in his stocking feet, puffing fiercely on his cigar as he warmed to the tale, blowing the smoke out through either ear, gesturing savagely, his face flushed and his eyes kindling.

"Well, now, lessee. First thing Our Mug does when he gets to Mazatlan is to communicate his arrival to Senora Estrada—telegraphs, you know; and, by the way, have him use a cipher."

"What kind of cipher?"

"Count three letters on from the right letter, see. If you were spelling *boat*, for instance, you would begin with an E, the third letter after B; then R for the O, being the third letter from O. So you'd spell *boat*, E-R-D-W; and Senora Estrada knows when she gets that despatch that she must count three letters *back* from each letter to get the right ones. Take now such a cipher word as U-L-I-O-H. That means *rifle*. Count three letters back from each letter of U-L-I-O-H, and it'll spell *rifle*. You can make up a lot of despatches like that, just to have the thing look natural; savvy?"

"Out of sight!" muttered Conde, making a note.

"Then Our Mug and Billy Isham start getting a crew. And Our Mug, he buys the sextant there in Mazatlan—the sextant, that got out of order and spoiled everything. Or, no; don't have it a sextant; have it a quadrant— an old-fashioned, ebony quadrant. Have Billy Isham buy it because it was cheap."

"How did it get out of order, Captain Jack?" inquired Blix. "That would be a good technical detail, wouldn't it, Conde?"

"Well, it's like this. Our Mug an' Billy get a schooner that's so bally small that they have to do their cooking in the cabin; quadrant's on a rack over the stove, and the heat warps the joints, so when Our Mug takes his observation he gets fifty miles off his course and raises the land where the government forces are watching for him."

"And here's another point, Cap.," said Conde. "We ought to work some kind of a treasure into this yarn; can't you think up something new and original in the way of a treasure? I don't want the old game of a buried chest of money. Let's have him get track of something that's worth a fortune—something novel."

"Yes, yes; I see the idea," answered the Captain, striding over the floor with great thuds of his stockinged feet. "Now, lessee; let me think," he began, rubbing all his hair the wrong way. "We want something new and queer, something that ain't ever been written up before. I tell you what! Here it is! Have Our Mug get wind of a little river schooner that sunk fifty years before his time in one of the big South American rivers, during a flood—I heard of this myself. Schooner went down and was buried twenty feet under mud and sand; and since that time—you know how the big rivers act—the whole blessed course of the river has changed at that point, and the schooner is on dry land, or rather twenty feet under it, and as sound as the day she was chartered."

"Well?"

"Well, have it that when she sank she had aboard of her a cargo of five hundred cases of whiskey, prime stuff, seven thousand quart bottles, sealed up tight as drums. Now Our Mug—nor Billy Isham either—they ain't born yesterday. No, sir; they're right next to themselves! They figure this way. This here whiskey's been kept fifty years without being moved. Now, what do you suppose seven thousand quart bottles of fifty-year-old whiskey would be worth? Why, twenty dollars a quart wouldn't be too fancy. So there you are; there's your treasure. Our Mug and Billy Isham have only got to dig through twenty feet of sand to pick up a hundred thousand dollars, *if they can find the schooner.*"

Blix clapped her hands with a little cry of delight, and Conde smote a knee, exclaiming:

"By Jove! That's as good as Loudon Dodds' opium ship! Why, Cap., you're a treasure in yourself for a fellow looking for stories."

Then after the notes were taken and the story talked over, Captain Jack, especially if the day happened to be Sunday, would insist upon their staying to dinner—boiled beef and cabbage. smoking coffee and pickles—that K. D. B. served in the little, brick-paved kitchen in the back of the station. The crew messed in their quarters overhead.

K. D. B. herself was not uninteresting. Her respectability incased her like armor plate, and she never laughed without putting three fingers to her lips. She told them that she had at one time been a "costume reader."

"A costume reader?"

"Yes; reading extracts from celebrated authors in the appropriate costume of the character. It used to pay very well, and it was very refined. I used to do *In a Balcony*, by Mister Browning, and *Laska*, the same evening! and it always made a hit. I'd do *In a Balcony* first, and I'd put on a Louis-Quinze-the-fifteenth gown and wig-to-match over a female cowboy outfit. When I'd finished *In a Balcony*, I'd do an exit, and shunt the gown and wig-to-match, and come on as *Laska*, with thunder noises off. It was one of the strongest effects in my repertoire, and it always got me a curtain call."

And Captain Jack would wag his head and murmur:

"Extraordinary! Extraordinary!"

Blix and Conde soon noted that upon the occasion of each one of their visits, K. D. B. found means to entertain them at great length with long discussions upon certain subjects of curiously diversified character. Upon their first visit she elected to talk upon the Alps mountains. The Sunday following it was bacteriology; on the next Wednesday it was crystals; while for two hours during their next visit to the station, Conde and

Blix were obliged to listen to K. D. B.'s interminable discourse on the origin, history, and development of the kingdom of Denmark. Conde was dumfounded.

"I never met such a person, man or woman, in all my life. Talk about education! Why, I think she knows everything!"

"In Defiance of Authority" soon began to make good progress, but Conde, once launched upon technical navigation, must have Captain Jack at his elbow continually, to keep him from foundering. In some sea novel he remembered to have come across the expression "garboard streak," and from the context guessed it was to be applied to a detail of a vessel's construction. In an unguarded moment he had written that his schooner's name "was painted in showy gilt letters upon her garboard streak."

"What's the garboard streak, Conde?" Blix had asked, when he had read the chapter to her.

"That's where they paint her name," he declared promptly. "I don't know exactly, but I like the sound of it."

But the next day, when he was reading this same chapter to Captain Jack, the latter suddenly interrupted with an exclamation as of acute physical anguish.

"What's that? Read that last over again," he demanded.

"'When they had come within a few boat's lengths,'" read Conde, "'they were able to read the schooner's name, painted in showy gilt letters upon her garboard streak.'"

"My God!" gasped the Captain, clasping his head. Then, with a shout: "Garboard streak! Garboard streak? Don't you know that the garboard streak is the last plank next the keel? You mean counter, not garboard streak. That regularly graveled me, that did!"

They stayed to dinner with the couple that afternoon, and for half an hour afterward K. D. B. told them of the wonders of the caves of Elephantis. One would have believed that she had actually been at the place. But when she changed the subject to the science of fortification, Blix could no longer restrain herself.

"But it is really wonderful that you should know all these things! Where did you find time to study so much?"

"One must have an education," returned K. D. B. primly.

But Conde had caught sight of a half-filled bookshelf against the opposite wall, and had been suddenly smitten with an inspiration. On a leaf of his notebook he wrote: "Try her on the G's and H's," and found means to show it furtively to Blix. But Blix was puzzled, and at the earliest opportunity Conde himself said to the retired costume reader:

"Speaking of fortifications, Mrs. Hoskins, Gibraltar now—that's a wonderful rock, isn't it?"

"Rock!" she queried. "I thought it was an island."

"Oh, no; it's a fortress. They have a castle there—a castle, something like—well, like the old Schloss at Heidelberg. Did you ever hear about or read about Heidelberg University?"

But K. D. B. was all abroad now. Gibraltar and Heidelberg were unknown subjects to her, as were also inoculation, Japan, and Kosciusko. Above the G's she was sound; below that point her ignorance was benighted.

"But what is it, Conde?" demanded Blix, as soon as they were alone.

"I've the idea," he answered, chuckling. "Wait till after Sunday to see if I'm right; then I'll tell you. It's a dollar to a paper dime, K. D. B. will have something for us by Sunday, beginning with an I."

And she had. It was Internal Revenue.

"Right! Right!" Conde shouted gleefully, as he and Blix were on their way home. "I knew it. She's done with Ash—Bol, Bol—Car, and all those, and has worked through Cod—Dem, and Dem—Eve. She's down to Hor—Kin now, and she'll go through the whole lot before she's done—Kin—Mag, Mag—Mot, Mot—Pal, and all the rest."

"The Encyclopaedia?"

"Don't you see it? No wonder she didn't know beans about Gibraltar! She hadn't come to the G's by then."

"She's reading the Encyclopaedia."

"And she gets the volumes on the installment plan, don't you see? Reads the leading articles, and then springs 'em on us. To know things and talk about 'em, that's her idea of being cultured. 'One must have an education.' Do you remember her saying that? Oh, our matrimonial objects are panning out beyond all expectation!"

What a delicious, never-to-be-forgotten month it was for those two! There in the midst of life they were as much alone as upon a tropic island. Blix had deliberately freed herself from a world that had grown distasteful to her; Conde little by little had dropped away from his place among the men and the women of his acquaintance, and the two came and went together, living in a little world of their own creation, happy in each other's society, living only in the present, and asking nothing better than to be left alone and to their own devices.

They saw each other every day. In the morning from nine till twelve, and in the afternoon until three, Conde worked away upon his novel, but not an evening passed that did not see him and Blix in the dining-room of the little flat. Thursdays and Sunday afternoons they visited the lifeboat station, and at other times prowled about the unfrequented corners of the city, now passing an afternoon along the water front, watching the departure of a China steamer or the loading of the great, steel wheat ships; now climbing the ladder-like streets of Telegraph Hill, or revisiting the Plaza, Chinatown, and the restaurant; or taking long walks in the Presidio Reservation, watching cavalry and artillery drills; or sitting for hours on the rocks by the seashore, watching the ceaseless roll and plunge of the surf, the wheeling sea-birds, and the sleek-headed seals hunting the offshore fish, happy for a half-hour when they surprised one with his prey in his teeth.

One day, some three weeks before the end of the year, toward two in the afternoon, Conde sat in his usual corner of the club, behind the screen, writing rapidly. His coat was off and the stump of a cigar was between his teeth. At his elbow was the rectangular block of his manuscript. During the last week the story had run from him with a facility that had surprised and delighted him; words came to him without effort, ranging themselves into line with the promptitude of well-drilled soldiery; sentences and paragraphs marched down the clean-swept spaces of his paper, like companies and platoons defiling upon review; his chapters were brigades that he marshaled at will, falling them in one behind the other, each preceded by its chapter-head, like an officer in the space between two divisions. In the guise of a commander-in-chief sitting his horse upon an eminence that overlooked the field of operations, Conde at last took in the entire situation at a glance, and, with the force and precision of a machine, marched his forces straight to the goal he had set for himself so long a time before.

Then at length he took a fresh penful of ink, squared his elbows, drew closer to the desk. and with a single swift spurt of the pen wrote the last line of his novel, dropping the pen upon the instant and pressing the blotter over the words as though setting a seal of approval upon the completed task.

"There!" he muttered, between his teeth; "I've done for *you*!"

That same afternoon he read the last chapter to Blix, and she helped him to prepare the manuscript for expressage. She insisted that it should go off that very day, and herself wrote the directions upon the outside wrapper. Then the two went down together to the Wells Fargo office, and "In Defiance of Authority" was sent on its journey across the continent.

"Now," she said, as they came out of the express office and stood for a moment upon the steps, "now there's nothing to do but wait for the Centennial Company. I do so hope we'll get their answer before I go away. They *ought* to take it. It's just what they asked for. Don't you think they'll take it, Conde?"

"Oh, bother that!" answered Conde. "I don't care whether they take it or not. How long now is it before you go, Blix?"

Chapter XIII

A week passed; then another. The year was coming to a close. In ten days Blix would be gone. Letters had been received from Aunt Kihm, and also an exquisite black leather traveling-case, a present to her niece, full of cut-glass bottles, ebony-backed brushes, and shell combs. Blix was to leave on the second day of January. In the meanwhile she had been reading far into her first-year textbooks, underscoring and annotating, studying for hours upon such subjects as she did not understand, so that she might get hold of her work the readier when it came to classroom routine and lectures. Hers was a temperament admirably suited to the study she had chosen—self-reliant, cool, and robust.

But it was not easy for her to go. Never before had Blix been away from her home; never for longer than a week had she been separated from her father, nor from Howard and Snooky. That huge city upon the Atlantic seaboard, with its vast, fierce life, where beat the heart of the nation, and where beyond Aunt Kihm she knew no friend, filled Blix with a vague sense of terror and of oppression. She was going out into a new life, a life of work and of study, a harsher life than she had yet known. Her father, her friends, her home—all these were to be left behind. It was not surprising that Blix should be daunted at the prospect of so great a change in her life, now so close at hand. But if the tears did start at times, no one ever saw them fall, and with a courage that was all her own Blix watched the last days of the year trooping past and the approach of the New Year that was to begin the new life.

But Conde was thoroughly unhappy. Those wonderful three months were at an end. Blix was going. In less than a week now she would be gone. He would see the last of her. Then what? He pictured himself—when he had said good-bye to her and the train had lessened to a smoky blur in the distance—facing about, facing the life that must then begin for him, returning to the city alone, picking up the routine again. There would be nothing to look forward to then; he would not see Blix in the afternoon; would not sit with her in the evening in the little dining-room of the flat overlooking the city and the bay; would not wake in the morning with the consciousness that before the sun would set he would see her again, be with her, and hear the sound of her voice. The months that were to follow would be one long ache, one long, harsh, colorless grind without her. How was he to get through that first evening that he must pass alone? And she did not care for him. Conde at last knew this to be so. Even the poor solace of knowing that she, too, was unhappy was denied him. She had never loved him, and never would. He was a chum to her, nothing more. Conde was too clear-headed to deceive himself upon this point. The time was come for her to go away, and she had given him no sign, no cue.

The last days passed; Blix's trunk was packed, her half section engaged, her ticket bought. They said good-bye to the old places they had come to know so well—Chinatown, the Golden Balcony, the waterfront, the lake of San Andreas, Telegraph Hill, and Luna's—and had bade farewell to Riccardo and to old Richardson. They had left K. D. B. and Captain Jack until the last day. Blix was to go on the second of January. On New Year's Day she and Conde were to take their last walk, were to go out to the lifeboat station, and then on around the shore to the little amphitheater of blackberry bushes—where they had promised always to write one another on the anniversary of their first visit—and then for the last time climb the hill, and go across the breezy downs to the city.

Then came the last day of the old year, the last day but one that they would be together. They spent it in a long ramble along the waterfront, fol-lowing the line of the shipping even as far as Meiggs's Wharf. They had come back to the flat for supper, and afterward, as soon as the family had left them alone, had settled themselves in the bay window to watch the New Year in.

The little dining-room was dark, but for the indistinct blur of light that came in through the window—a light that was a mingling of the after-glow, the new-risen moon, and the faint haze that the city threw off into the sky from its street lamps and electrics. From where they sat they could look down, almost as from a tower, into the city's streets. Here a corner came into view; further on a great puff of green foliage—palms and pines side by side—overlooked a wall. Here a street was visible for almost its entire length, like a stream of asphalt flowing down the pitch of the hill, dammed on either side by rows upon rows of houses; while further on the vague con-fusion of roofs and facades opened out around a patch of green lawn, the garden of some larger residence.

As they looked and watched, the afterglow caught window after window, till all that quarter of the city seemed to stare up at them from a thousand ruddy eyes. The windows seemed infinite in number, the streets endless in their complications: yet everything was deserted. At this hour the streets were empty, and would remain so until daylight. Not a soul was stirring; no face looked from any of those myriads of glowing windows; no footfall disturbed the silence of those asphalt streets. There, almost within call behind those windows, shut off from those empty streets, a thousand human lives were teeming, each the center of its own circle of thoughts and words and actions; and yet the solitude was profound, the desolation complete. the stillness unbroken by a single echo.

The night—the last night of the old year—was fine; the white, clear light from a moon they could not see grew wide and clear over the city, as the last gleam of the sunset faded. It was just warm enough for the window to be open, and for nearly three hours Conde and Blix sat looking down upon the city in these last moments of the passing year, feeling upon their faces an occasional touch of the breeze, that carried with it the smell of trees and flowers from the gardens below them, and the faint fine taint of the ocean from far out beyond the Heads. But the scene was not in reality silent. At times when they listened intently, especially when they closed their eyes, there came to them a subdued, steady bourdon, profound, unceasing, a vast, numb murmur, like no other sound in all the gamut of nature—the sound of a city at night, the hum of a great, conglomerate life, wrought out there from moment to moment under the stars and under the moon, while the last hours of the old year dropped quietly away.

A star fell.

Sitting in the window, the two noticed it at once, and Conde stirred for the first time in fifteen minutes.

"That was a very long one," he said, in a low voice. "Blix, you must write to me—we must write each other often."

"Oh, yes," she answered. "We must not forget each other; we have had too good a time for that."

"Four years is a long time," he went on. "Lots can happen in four years. Wonder what I'll be doing at the end of four years? We've had a pleasant time while it lasted, Blix."

"Haven't we?" she said, her chin on her hand, the moonlight shining in her little, dark-brown eyes.

Well, he was going to lose her. He had found out that he loved her only in time to feel the wrench of parting from her all the more keenly. What was he to do with himself after she was gone? What could he turn to in order to fill up the great emptiness that her going would leave in his daily life? And was she never to know how dear she was to him? Why not speak to her, why not tell her that he loved her? But Conde knew that Blix did not love him, and the knowledge of that must keep him silent; he must hug his secret to him, like the Spartan boy with his stolen fox, no matter how grievously it hurt him to do so. He and Blix had lived through two months of rarest, most untroubled happiness, with hardly more self-consciousness than two young and healthy boys. To bring that troublous, disquieting element of love between them—unrequited love, of all things—would be a folly. She would tell him—must in all honesty tell him that she did not love him, and all their delicious camaraderie would end in a "scene." Conde, above everything, wished to look back on those two months, after she had gone, without being able to remember therein one single note that jarred. If the memory of her was all that he was to have, he resolved that at least that memory should be perfect.

And the love of her had made a man of him—he could not forget that; had given to him just the strength that made it possible for him to keep that resolute, grim silence now. In those two months he had grown five years; he was more masculine, more virile. The very set of his mouth was different; between the eyebrows the cleft had deepened; his voice itself vibrated to a heavier note. No, no; so long as he should live, he, man grown as he was, could never forget this girl of nineteen who had come into his life so quietly, so unexpectedly, who had influenced it so irresistibly and so unmistakably for its betterment, and who had passed out of it with the passing of the year.

For a few moments Conde had been absentmindedly snapping the lid of his cigarette case, while he thought; now he selected a cigarette, returned the case to his pocket, and fumbled for a match. But the little gun-metal case he carried was empty. Blix rose and groped for a moment upon the mantel-shelf, then returned and handed him a match, and stood over him while he scraped it under the arm of the chair wherein he sat. Even when his cigarette was lighted she still stood there, looking at him, the fingers of her hands clasped in front of her, her hair, one side of her cheek, her chin, and sweet, round neck outlined by the faint blur of light that came from the open window. Then quietly she said:

"Well, Conde?"

"Well, Blix?"

"Just 'well'?" she repeated. "Is that all? Is that all you have to say to me?"

He gave a great start.

"Blix!" he exclaimed.

"Is that all? And you are going to let me go away from you for so long, and say nothing more than that to me? You think you have been so careful, think you have kept your secret so close! Conde, don't you suppose I know? Do you suppose women are so blind? No, you don't need to tell me;

I know—I've known it—oh, for weeks!"

"You know—know—know what?" he exclaimed, breathless.

"That you have been pretending that you did not love me. I know that you do love me—I know you have been trying to keep it from me for fear it would spoil our good times, and because we had made up our minds to be chums, and have 'no more foolishness.' Once—in those days when we first knew each other—I knew you did not love me when you said you did; but now, since—oh, since that afternoon in the Chinese restaurant, remember?—I've known that you did love me, although you pretended you didn't. It was the pretense I wanted to be rid of; I wanted to be rid of it when you said you loved me and didn't, and I want to be rid of it now when *you* pretend not to love me and I *know* you do," and Blix leaned back her head as she spoke that "know," looking at him from under her lids, a smile upon her lips. "It's the pretense that I won't have," she added. "We must be sincere with each other, you and I."

"Blix, do *you* love *me?*"

Conde had risen to his feet, his breath was coming quick, his cigarette was flung away, and his hands opened and shut swiftly.

"Oh, Blixy, little girl, do *you* love *me?*"

They stood there for a moment in the half dark, facing one another, their hearts beating, their breath failing them in the tension of the instant. There in that room, high above the city, a little climax had come swiftly to a head, a crisis in two lives had suddenly developed. The moment that had been in preparation for the last few months, the last few years, the last few centuries, behold! It had arrived.

"Blix, do you love me?"

Suddenly it was the New Year. Somewhere close at hand a chorus of chiming church bells sang together. Far off in the direction of the wharves, where the great ocean steamships lay, came the glad, sonorous shouting of a whistle; from a nearby street a bugle called aloud. And then from point to point, from street to roof top, and from roof to spire, the vague murmur of many sounds grew and spread and widened, slowly, grandly; that profound and steady bourdon, as of an invisible organ swelling, deepening, and expanding to the full male diapason of the city aroused and signaling the advent of another year.

And they heard it, they two heard it, standing there face to face, looking into each other's eyes, that unanswered question yet between them, the question that had come to them with the turning of the year. It was the old year yet when Conde had asked that question. In that moment's pause, while Blix hesitated to answer him, the New Year had come. And while the huge, vast note of the city swelled and vibrated, she still kept silent. But only for a moment. Then she came closer to him, and put a hand on each of his shoulders.

"Happy New Year, dear," she said.

*   *   *

On New Year's Day, the last day they were to be together, Blix and Conde took "their walk," as they had come to call it—the walk that included the lifeboat station, the Golden Gate, the ocean beach beyond the old fort, the green, bare, flower-starred hills and downs, and the smooth levels of the golf links. Blix had been busy with the last details of her packing, and they did not get started until toward two in the afternoon.

"Strike me!" exclaimed Captain Jack, as Blix informed him that she had come to say good-bye. "Why, ain't this very sudden-like, Miss Bessemer? Hey, Kitty, come in here. Here's Miss Bessemer come to say good-bye; going to New York tomorrow."

"We'll regularly be lonesome without you, miss," said K. D. B., as she came into the front room, bringing with her a brisk, pungent odor of boiled vegetables. "New York—such a town as it must be! It was called Manhattan at first, you know, and was settled by the Dutch."

Evidently K. D. B. had reached the N's.

With such deftness as she possessed, Blix tried to turn the conversation upon the first meeting of the retired sea captain and the onetime costume reader, but all to no purpose. The "Matrimonial Objects" were perhaps a little ashamed of their "personals" by now, and neither Blix nor Conde were ever to hear their version of the meeting in the back dining-room of Luna's Mexican restaurant. Captain Jack was, in fact, anxious to change the subject.

"Any news of the yarn yet?" he suddenly inquired of Conde "What do those Eastern publishin' people think of Our Mug and Billy Isham and the whiskey schooner?"

Conde had received the rejected manuscript of "In Defiance of Authority" that morning, accompanied by a letter from the Centennial Company.

"Well," he said in answer, "they're not, as you might say, falling over themselves trying to see who'll be the first to print it. It's been returned."

"The devil you say!" responded the Captain. "Well, that's kind of disappointin' to you, ain't it?"

"But," Blix hastened to add, "we're not at all discouraged. We're going to send it off again right away."

Then she said good-bye to them.

"I dunno as you'll see me here when you come back, miss," said the Captain, at the gate, his arm around K. D. B. "I've got to schemin' again. Do you know," he added, in a low, confidential tone, "that all the mines in California send their clean-ups and gold bricks down to the Selby smeltin' works once every week? They send 'em to San Francisco first, and they are taken up to Selby's Wednesday afternoons on a little stern-wheel steamer called the *Monticello*. All them bricks are in a box—dumped in like so much coal—and that box sets just under the wheel-house, for'ard. How much money do you suppose them bricks represent? Well, I'll tell you; last week they represented seven hundred and eighty thousand dollars. Well, now, I got a chart of the bay near Vallejo; the channel's all right, but there are mudflats that run out from shore three miles. Enough water for a white-hall, but not enough for—well, for the patrol boat, for instance. Two or three slick boys, of a foggy night—of course, I'm not in that kind of game, but strike! It would be a deal now, wouldn't it?"

"Don't you believe him, miss," put in K. D. B. "He's just talking to show off."

"I think your scheme of holding up a Cunard liner," said Conde, with great earnestness, "is more feasible. You could lay across her course and fly a distress signal. She'd have to heave to."

"Yes, I been thinkin' o' that; but look here—what's to prevent the liner taking right after your schooner after you've got the stuff aboard—just followin' you right around an' findin' out where you land?"

"She'd be under contract to carry Government mails," contradicted Conde. "She couldn't do that. You'd leave her mails aboard for just that reason. You wouldn't rob her of her mails; just so long as she was carrying government mails she couldn't stop."

The Captain clapped his palm down upon the gate-post.

"Strike me straight! I never thought of that."

Chapter XIV

Blix and Conde went on; on along the narrow road upon the edge of the salt marshes and tules that lay between the station and the Golden Gate; on to the Golden Gate itself, and around the old grime-incrusted fort to the ocean shore, with its reaches of hard, white sand, where the boulders lay tumbled and the surf grumbled incessantly.

The world seemed very far away from them here on the shores of the Pacific, on that first afternoon of the New Year. They were supremely happy, and they sufficed to themselves. Conde had forgotten all about the next day, when he must say good-bye to Blix.

It did not seem possible, it was not within the bounds of possibility, that she was to go away—that they two were to be separated. And for that matter, tomorrow was tomorrow. It was twenty-four hours away. The present moment was sufficient.

The persistence with which they clung to the immediate moment, their happiness in living only in the present, had brought about a rather curious condition of things between them.

In their love for each other there was no thought of marriage; they were too much occupied with the joy of being together at that particular instant to think of the future. They loved each other, and that was enough. They did not look ahead further than the following day, and then but fur-tively, and only in order that their morrow's parting might intensify their happiness of today. That New Year's Day was to be the end of everything. Blix was going; she and Conde would never see each other again. The thought of marriage—with its certain responsibilities, its duties, its gravity, its vague, troublous seriousness, its inevitable disappointments—was even a little distasteful to them. Their romance had been hitherto without a flaw; they had been genuinely happy in little things. It was as well that it should end that day, in all its pristine sweetness, unsullied by a single bitter moment, undimmed by the cloud of a single disillusion or disappoint-ment. Whatever chanced to them in later years, they could at least cherish this one memory of a pure, unselfish affection, young and unstained and almost without thought of sex, come and gone on the very threshold of their lives. This was the end, they both understood. They were glad that it was to be so. They did not even speak again of writing to each other.

They found once more the little semicircle of blackberry bushes and the fallen log, halfway up the hill above the shore, and sat there a while, looking down upon the long green rollers, marching incessantly toward the beach, and there breaking in a prolonged explosion of solid green water and flying spume. And their glance followed their succeeding ranks further and further out to sea, till the multitude blended into the mass—the vast, green, shifting mass that drew the eye on and on, to the abrupt, fine line of the horizon.

There was no detail in the scene. There was nothing but the great reach of the ocean floor, the unbroken plane of blue sky, and the bare green slope of land—three immensities, gigantic, vast, primordial. It was no place for trivial ideas and thoughts of little things. The mind harked back unconsciously to the broad, simpler, basic emotions, the fundamental instincts of the race. The huge spaces of earth and air and water carried with them a feeling of kindly but enormous force—elemental force, fresh, untutored, new, and young. There was buoyancy in it; a fine, breathless sense of uplifting and exhilaration; a sensation as of bigness and a return to the homely, human, natural life, to the primitive old impulses, irresistible, changeless, and unhampered; old as the ocean, stable as the hills, vast as the unplumbed depths of the sky.

Conde and Blix sat still, listening, looking, and watching—the intellect drowsy and numb; the emotions, the senses, all alive and brimming to the surface. Vaguely they felt the influence of the moment. Something was preparing for them. From the lowest, untouched depths in the hearts of each of them something was rising steadily to consciousness and the light of day. There is no name for such things, no name for the mystery that spans the interval between man and woman—the mystery that bears no relation to their love for each other, but that is something better than love, and whose coming savors of the miraculous.

The afternoon had waned and the sun had begun to set when Blix rose.

"We should be going, Conde," she told him.

They started up the hill, and Conde said: "I feel as though I had been somehow asleep with my eyes wide open. What a glorious sunset! It seems to me as though I were living double every minute; and oh! Blix, isn't it the greatest thing in the world to love each other as we do?"

They had come to the top of the hill by now, and went on across the open, breezy downs, all starred with blue iris and wild heliotrope. Blix drew his arm about her waist, and laid her cheek upon his shoulder with a little caressing motion.

"And I do love you, dear," she said—"love you with all my heart. And it's for always, too; I know that. I've been a girl until within the last three or four days—just a girl, dearest; not very serious, I'm afraid, and not caring for anything else beyond, what was happening close around me—don't you understand? But since I've found out how much I loved you and knew that you loved me—why, everything is changed for me. I'm not the same, I enjoy things that I never thought of enjoying before, and I feel so—oh, *larger*, don't you know?—and stronger, and so much more serious. Just a little while ago I was only nineteen, but I think, dear, that by loving you I have become—all of a sudden and without knowing it—a woman."

A little trembling ran through her with the words. She stopped and put both arms around his neck, her head tipped back, her eyes half closed, her sweet yellow hair rolling from her forehead. Her whole dear being radiated with that sweet, clean perfume that seemed to come alike from her clothes, her neck, her arms, her hair, and mouth—the delicious, almost divine, feminine aroma that was part of herself.

"You do love me, Conde, don't you, just as I love you?"

Such words as he could think of seemed pitifully inadequate. For answer he could only hold her the closer. She understood. Her eyes closed slowly, and her face drew nearer to his. Just above a whisper, she said:

"I love you, dear!"

"I love you, Blix!"

And they kissed each other then upon the mouth.

Meanwhile the sun had been setting. Such a sunset! The whole world, the three great spaces of sea and land and sky, were incarnadined with the glory of it. The ocean floor was a blinding red radiance, the hills were amethyst, the sky one gigantic opal, and they two seemed poised in the midst of all the chaotic glory of a primitive world. It was New Year's Day; the earth was new, the year was new, and their love was new and strong. Everything was before them. There was no longer any past, no longer any present. Regrets and memories had no place in their new world. It was Hope, Hope, Hope, that sang to them and called to them and smote into life the new keen blood of them.

Then suddenly came the miracle, like the flashing out of a new star, whose radiance they felt but could not see, like a burst of music whose harmony they felt but could not hear. And as they stood there alone in all that simple glory of sky and earth and sea, they knew all in an instant that *they were for each other*, forever and forever, for better or for worse, till death should them part. Into their romance, into their world of little things, their joys of the moment, their happiness of the hour, had suddenly descended a great and lasting joy, the happiness of the great, grave issues of life—a happiness so deep, so intense, as to thrill them with a sense of solemnity and wonder. Instead of being the end, that New Year's Day was but the beginning—the beginning of their real romance. All the fine, virile, masculine energy of him was aroused and rampant. All her sweet, strong womanliness had been suddenly deepened and broadened. In fine, he had become a man, and she woman. Youth, life, and the love of man and woman, the strength of the hills, the depth of the ocean, and the beauty of the sky at sunset; that was what the New Year had brought to them.

*   *   *

"It's good-bye, dear, isn't it?" said Blix.

But Conde would not have it so.

"No, no," he told her; "no, Blix; no matter how often we separate after this wonderful New Year's Day, no matter how far we are apart, *we* two shall never, never say good-bye."

"Oh, you're right, you're right!" she answered, the tears beginning to shine in her little dark-brown eyes. "No; so long as we love each other, nothing matters. There's no such thing as distance for us, is there? Just think, you will be here on the shores of the Pacific, and I on the shores of the Atlantic, but the whole continent can't come between *us*."

"And we'll be together again, Blix," he said; "and it won't be very long now. Just give me time—a few years now."

"But so long as we love each other, *time* won't matter either."

"What are the tears for, Blixy?" he asked, pressing his handkerchief to her cheek.

"Because this is the saddest and happiest day of my life," she answered. Then she pulled from him with a little laugh, adding: "Look, Conde, you've dropped your letter. You pulled it out just now with your handkerchief."

As Conde picked it up, she noted the name of the Centennial Company upon the corner.

"It's the letter I got with the manuscript of the novel when they sent it back," he explained.

"What did they say?"

"Oh, the usual thing. I haven't read it yet. Here's what they say." He opened it and read:

> We return to you herewith the MS. of your novel, *In Defiance of Authority*, and regret that our reader does not recommend it as available for publication at present. We have, however, followed your work

with considerable interest, and have read a story by you, copied in one of our exchanges, under the title, *A Victory Over Death,* which we would have been glad to publish ourselves, had you given us the chance.

Would you consider the offer of the assistant editorship of our *Quarterly,* a literary and critical pamphlet, that we publish in New York, and with which we presume you are familiar? We do not believe there would be any difficulty in the matter of financial arrangements. In case you should decide to come on, we inclose R. R. passes via the A. T. & S. F., C. & A., and New York Central.

Very truly,
THE CENTENNIAL PUBLISHING COMPANY,
NEW YORK.

The two exchanged glances. But Blix was too excited to speak, and could only give vent to a little, quivering, choking sigh. The letter was a veritable god from the machine, the one thing lacking to complete their happiness.

"I don't know how this looks to you," Conde began, trying to be calm, "but it seems to me that this is—that this—this—"

But what they said then they could never afterward remember. The golden haze of the sunset somehow got into their recollection of the moment, and they could only recall the fact that they had been gayer in that moment than ever before in all their lives.

Perhaps as gay as they ever were to be again. They began to know the difference between gaiety and happiness. That New Year's Day, that sunset, marked for them an end and a beginning. It was the end of their gay, irresponsible, hour-to-hour life of the past three months; and it was the beginning of a new life, whose possibilities of sorrow and of trouble, of pleasure and of happiness, were greater than aught they had yet experienced. They knew this—they felt it instinctively, as with a common impulse they turned and looked back upon the glowing earth and sea and sky, the breaking surf, the beach, the distant, rime-incrusted, ancient fort—all that scene that to their eyes stood for the dear, free, careless companionship of those last few months. Their newfound happiness was not without its sadness already. All was over now; their solitary walks, the long, still evenings in the little dining-room overlooking the sleeping city, their excursions to Luna's, their afternoons spent in the golden Chinese balcony, their mornings on the lake, calm and still and hot. Forever and forever they had said good-bye to that life. Already the sunset was losing its glory.

Then, with one last look, they turned about and set their faces from it to the new life, to the East, where lay the Nation. Out beyond the purple bulwarks of the Sierras, far off, the great, grim world went clashing through its grooves—the world that now they were to know, the world that called to them, and woke them, and roused them. Their little gaieties were done; the life of little things was all behind. Now for the future. The sterner note had struck—work was to be done; that, too, the New Year had brought to them—work for each of them, work and the world of men.

For a moment they shrank from it, loth to take the first step beyond the confines of the garden wherein they had lived so joyously and learned to love each other; and as they stood there, facing the gray and darkening Eastern sky, their backs forever turned to the sunset, Blix drew closer to him, putting her hand in his, looking a little timidly into his eyes. But his arm was around her, and the strong young force that looked into her eyes from his gave her courage.

"A happy New Year, dear," she said.

"A very, very happy New Year, Blix," he answered.

The End

www.ingramcontent.com/pod-product-compliance
Lightning Source LLC
Chambersburg PA
CBHW052149170626
46812CB00004B/1657